Sue MacKay lives with her husband in New Zealand's beautiful Marlborough Sounds, with the water on her doorstep and the birds and the trees at her back door. It is the perfect setting to indulge her passions of entertaining friends by cooking them sumptuous meals, drinking fabulous wine, going for hill walks or kayaking around the bay—and, of course, writing stories.

Also by Sue MacKay

Their Second Chance in ER
Fling with Her Long-Lost Surgeon
Stranded with the Paramedic
Single Mum's New Year Wish
Brought Together by a Pup
Fake Fiancée to Forever?

Queenstown Search & Rescue miniseries

Captivated by Her Runaway Doc
A Single Dad to Rescue Her
From Best Friend to I Do?

Discover more at millsandboon.co.uk.

RESISTING THE PREGNANT PAEDIATRICIAN

SUE MacKAY

MILLS & BOON

First published in Great Britain 2023
by Mills & Boon, an imprint of HarperCollins*Publishers* Ltd,
1 London Bridge Street, London, SE1 9GF

www.harpercollins.co.uk

HarperCollins*Publishers*
Macken House, 39/40 Mayor Street Upper,
Dublin 1, D01 C9W8, Ireland

Large Print edition 2024

ISBN: 978-0-263-31191-4

05/24

FSC
www.fsc.org
MIX
Paper | Supporting responsible forestry
FSC™ C007454

This book contains FSC™ certified paper and other controlled sources to ensure responsible forest management.

For more information visit www.harpercollins.co.uk/green.

Printed and Bound in the UK using 100% Renewable Electricity
at CPI Group (UK) Ltd, Croydon, CR0 4YY

This book is for my good friend
Vicki Rule.
There are days I'd go bonkers
if we couldn't have a wine together.

CHAPTER ONE

'WATCH OUT, YOU IDIOT!' Bella Rosso shouted at the car speeding past.

The driver cut in front of her.

She swore as she slammed her foot on the brake to avoid a collision. 'Some people shouldn't be allowed behind a steering wheel.'

The sun was on its slow descent towards the horizon and the road between Lake Orta and Stresa was busy with people heading home after work. Not a time for any driver to be pushing their way through the traffic. No time was right for that, Bella admitted, jerking forward when her car came to an abrupt stop.

The vehicle causing problems swerved back towards the centre of the road, then veered straight into a small cyclist on a child-sized bike. Make that cyclists plural.

Heart leaping to her throat, Bella eased her car off the road before leaping out to run over to the two small boys lying entangled in the bike frame and wheels. Shock stared up at her from their little faces. 'Hello, boys.' At least, she thought they were boys with their messy short haircuts and tee shirts with trucks on the front. 'I'm a doctor. I'm going to help you, all right?' She was already on her knees beside them, ascertaining the situation. 'Don't try to move until I say so. You might hurt yourselves even more.'

One began crying. 'The car hit us. We didn't do anything wrong.'

'I know. Let me check you over before we worry about that.' She looked around and saw other people racing towards them. 'Someone call the *polizia* and an ambulance.'

'The police are already here. They were on the other side of the roundabout watching the traffic when this happened,' a woman informed her.

'Hope that means they know what went down,' Bella said, half to herself. Because the driver of the car *had* been negligent, the driving shocking.

A man crouched down on the other side of the boys. A steal-her-breath-away kind of man. So good-looking, he couldn't be for real.

'I'm a doctor,' he said, bringing her back on track.

Just as well since there were *two* injured boys to concentrate on helping.

'Good. The more the better. I'm also a doctor.' Then she added for good measure, so he understood that she knew what she was about, 'A paediatrician.'

'Emergency specialist.' He was already carefully moving one boy's arm from between the steering bar and the asphalt path.

'The boys are in good hands, then.'

'You're local?' There was an intriguing accent emphasising his Italian words. Possibly British but she couldn't tell where from, which was odd considering she'd lived and worked in London for four years.

'Yes.' She felt over the head of the other boy.

'I'm currently working at the Stresa Hospital,' he told her.

Was this the temporary emergency specialist she'd heard was meant to start this week while she'd been working in Milano? More than likely, it was, which meant that from what she'd heard about him the accent was from Scotland.

A woman suddenly shouted, 'Out of the way! I'm a nurse, I'll see to the children.'

The new doctor stood up, wariness all over his face. 'Easy does it.'

'They rode their bike in front of my car. It's their fault this happened.'

Something hard stabbed Bella's shoulder, sending her falling sideways. *Not exactly how I saw the accident unfolding*, she thought as she struggled to right herself.

'Hey, look out.' The wariness changed to annoyance as the doctor stepped between her and the ranting woman. 'Move away. Don't hurt anyone else,' he snapped.

'Not my fault the stupid boys rode in front of me.' The ranting woman tried stepping around him again.

'Lady, move back now.' He stepped with her to prevent the woman getting anywhere near Bella or the boys. She could see he was tense, as if he was expecting trouble. But he was probably used to that if he worked in emergency departments. When the fuming woman didn't move he turned his back on her and reached down to help Bella. 'Here, give me your hand.'

Looking up—a long way up—she nodded.

'Thanks.' One firm tug and she was on her feet, rubbing her shoulder where a small throb had set up.

'Let me through,' the woman shouted again, her arms flailing in all directions, coming up against the doctor's firm stance, whacking his arm.

Bella stepped back, but was too late to avoid knuckles striking her in the side. She gasped. 'Hey.' Her hand immediately reached for her abdomen. There was a baby in there.

'Stop that,' the Scotsman snapped, again stepping between Bella and the apparent mad-woman. 'We're doctors and will look after the boys. Please move away. We don't need your help.' He looked around, and called out to the two policemen heading their way. 'Can you remove this woman? She's getting in the way of us seeing to the lads.' He wasn't hesitant in expressing his annoyance and was being protective of her and the boys. He'd definitely come face to face with difficult people before, she'd say.

His accent sent an unexpected thrill down Bella's spine. Totally inappropriate. As well as unasked for. Besides, right now it was the boys needing her attention, not her quiet, steady life. Kneeling down, she returned to looking after the kids, who were shaking and pale. 'It's all right, boys. You're going to be okay. What are your names?'

Her hands were moving up and down the left leg of one lad who, having been on the back of the bike, would've taken the brunt of the knock from the car, from what she'd seen. *Sì*, as she suspected, a fracture to the femur. Getting him free of the wheel wasn't going to be easy, or comfortable. 'Need painkillers fast,' she said aloud.

Neither of the boys had answered with their names. No doubt too shocked to understand what was going on.

'Fractured?' asked her counterpart as he concentrated on the second boy.

'Sì.' When in Italy speak Italian, even if she was fluent in English and this man's first language would be English. 'Have the police removed the woman?'

'Yes.' He nodded. 'There's a definite alcohol smell emanating from her.'

'Her driving was dangerous moments before she hit these two.'

'You saw what happened?'

'I did.' She'd talk to the police once the boys were hospital bound. 'I was behind her, and had to brake to avoid being hit.' She couldn't imagine the outcome had she taken the hit in her car instead of these two but they would probably still be happily biking along the side of the road.

The man opposite her was ever so gently moving the front wheel just enough to feel along the other kid's legs, quite the opposite to his manner with the deranged driver who'd caused the accident. 'Fracture in the lower leg.' He looked around as a siren cut through the chatter going on behind them. 'Not before time.'

Talk about impatient. 'That's a fast response,' Bella told him. It couldn't have been many minutes since the call went to 112.

'You're right. It's just that I always hold my breath in serious situations until an ambulance arrives,' he said quietly.

Something she could relate to. One time the ambulance had been too late for the man she was trying to stabilise after a cardiac arrest. Incidents like that never left her.

'Mamma,' finally screamed the boy she was looking after.

Running her hand over his right arm that appeared free of injury, Bella spoke softly. 'Mamma's not here but the policeman will bring her to see you at the hospital.' They needed some info to go on. The boys were wearing the local school's uniform, which was a start. Names would help a lot more. 'What's your name?'

'An-Andrea.' Tears streamed down the sides of his face. 'I want Mamma.'

Her heart was breaking for him. This had to be so frightening. Surrounded with people he didn't recognise, his mother not here to make him feel better, and then there was the pain and shock. If only she could lift him into her arms and hug away all the trauma. Instead she went with smoothing back the hair stuck to his forehead. 'What's your friend's name?'

'Mattia.'

The other boy was lying still, eyes closed, his breathing rapid and shallow.

'Can you hear me, Mattia?' the ED specialist asked. 'I'm Aaron, a doctor.'

The boy slowly opened his eyes, but said nothing.

Aaron. Come to think of it, she might have heard that name mentioned before. 'I'm glad they were wearing helmets,' she said. The consequences of being slammed into the pavement could've been far worse. Not that either of them would be cycling for a while to come. 'We need some serious painkillers here, otherwise extricating these two from the bike is going to be unbearable.' Not happening on her watch.

'Agreed.' Aaron looked around. 'Help's arrived.'

Within moments paramedics had taken over and were administering drugs to numb the pain before putting both boys on oxygen, then she and Aaron helped remove them from the mangled cycle to place them on stretchers.

Finally she was able to stand up straight, only to wince as a sharp pain stabbed her in the side. Her hand hovered over her abdomen. That woman had better not have hurt her baby. That would really get her wound up and on the warpath. Not that she'd be able to do a thing about it. But she wanted this baby so badly the mere idea of losing it made her blood boil.

Jason might not be alive to meet his child, but she would do all in her power to make up for his absence. It had taken nearly three years for her to finally feel ready to have in vitro insemination and nothing, nobody, was going to get in the way of this pregnancy going full term.

'You all right?' Aaron stood in front of her, looking concerned.

'I'm fine, thank you.' But very angry.

Calm down, Bella. A smack in the side isn't likely to jeopardise your baby.

True. She did get a bit paranoid about her pregnancy at times. Doing it alone got her uptight whenever the slightest little thing went wrong. She chose not to download her worry on anyone, which got a bit lonely at times. While her family hovered over her pretty much non-stop, she didn't like to tell any of them her fears about something going wrong with the pregnancy. They'd only get even more determined to keep her wrapped up in cotton wool, and she was well and truly over that. Since Jason died she'd slowly got back on her feet and begun facing life again, and now she was not going back to that dark, sad place ever again.

'You sure?' The doctor was watching her

very closely. Too closely for someone who didn't know her. There was nothing but concern in his face, but still. He didn't need to know about her pregnancy. Or her OTT worries.

But why was he so concerned?

She didn't need his concern on top of everyone else's in her life right now. 'Yes. What about you?'

'I'm fine.'

'Thank you for intervening with that woman. She was definitely on a mission.' Bella looked around for the police. She'd go and fill them in on the details of the accident she'd witnessed. Accident? Really? When the woman had been going too fast and was obviously under the influence? Technically the incident would be written up as an accident, but she'd seen the results of so-called accidents far too often during her medical training to think of them as anything other than bad decision-making with horrendous consequences for innocent people. 'I'll talk to the police about what happened.'

'I'm Aaron Marshall, and here for the next four months.' He held his hand out. 'I'm sure we'll see a bit of each other at the hospital. It's not exactly a huge place.' His smile had become warm and full of confidence, like a man used to getting his own way over just about anything and everything. Especially if he used that smile.

Well, it wasn't getting to her. She was immune to charming men. Jason had been the love of her life, and there wouldn't be another one of those hanging around for her. No one got two goes at such a deep love.

'I'm sure we will.' She shook his hand briefly, then stepped back, needing to put a hold on the sudden heat that flared between their hands. 'Bella Rosso. Nice to meet you.'

That suck-her-in smile remained. 'Not in the best of circumstances.'

'No.' She turned around to head for the policewoman talking to a man on the side of the road. There was no need to hang around being polite with Aaron. As he said, they'd bump into each other at work. That was enough. He might be intriguing with that spine-tingling accent and tall build—*why did tall men turn her on?*—but her future was mapped out and it did not include getting involved with the temporary ED doc.

Or any man, for that matter. She'd loved Jason with all her heart, and couldn't imagine loving another man as much. So far, the three dates she had gone on in the last year to shut her family down about getting out there again had been enjoyable but not filled with heat and passion. Pleasant, not exciting. More about pretending to be having a full life so her family backed off.

Unfortunately those dates had only endorsed the fact the love she'd known with her late husband had been special and rare and wasn't going to be repeated. Now she had her wonderful career, and a baby to bring into the world and raise the best she could. Along with help and understanding from her three bossy brothers and parents who often hinted she shouldn't be doing this alone.

Tough. She was. Nothing was going to change that. Nothing and nobody. In the last weeks of Jason's life they'd talked for hours about her having their baby when he was gone. He'd been concerned that she might not cope alone while working at the career she'd always dreamed about, but he'd also made it very clear it would be amazing if she did go ahead. She'd pointed out that if she hadn't miscarried months earlier she'd already be facing parenting on her own. She couldn't make him any promises about going ahead with a pregnancy, even if deep down she knew she would have his baby. Their baby. It was a way to keep Jason with her. She didn't regret it at all.

It was too late for regrets, anyway.

Aaron pulled into Gino's *ristorante* car park and turned off the car. Linguine and a glass of Pinot Grigio was what he needed after a busy day in ED followed by that accident with the two kids knocked off their bike. He wasn't allowing any thoughts of Dr Bella Rosso into the mix. Not even how she'd turned her back on him and walked across to the officer to talk about what she'd seen go down when the car took out those boys.

Sure, she'd been doing the right thing, but she didn't have to be so abrupt with him. He was only being open and friendly, which usually won most women over.

Did he want to win over this particular one? Why? Partly because she hadn't dropped to her knees at the sight of him as so many women usually did. Because of his famous family, his face and name went before him and made life tedious when it came to keeping clout-chasing women at bay. So far that hadn't happened here in Italy but he knew it was only a matter of time.

No denying a fling to while away the hours when he wasn't at work would be fun and would help him relax some, might even help him sleep a little at night. Plus it would add to his Italian experience. He sensed Bella wasn't going to be the one to make his nights pass in enjoyment and help him get his mojo back. She was a bit too serious for his taste.

You were at an accident scene. Of course she was serious.

There hadn't been any smiles forthcoming afterwards though.

She still had to talk to the police.

Seeing those two little guys slammed into by a car had probably wiped any thought of a smile off her lovely face. Plus the way that woman shoved her out of the way with no consideration for anyone else whatsoever. His initial reaction had been fear she might attack him or the paediatrician—a serious attack like the one that nearly took his life back in Edinburgh—but he'd quickly reclaimed his composure, and the need to protect had kicked in fast, as per normal. He'd been too late to prevent Dr Bella falling to the ground. He ground his teeth. What was that other woman on? He thought he'd smelt alcohol but could be wrong. She might just be OTT. Guess he'd never know, and didn't really need to. But the stunned look on Bella's face as she fell remained with him. He hadn't caught her in time.

'Give it a break,' Aaron muttered and shoved the car door open. He didn't need any hassles. He was here to get back up to speed after a galling incident back in Edinburgh. His left hand automatically rubbed the top of his thigh where the knife had sliced through the artery. Attacked by a drugged-up patient during an extremely disorderly night in the emergency department back home, he'd been lucky to survive. The blood loss had been serious to the point he wouldn't have made it if he hadn't been in the centre of the department with all the equipment and staff to deal with such an emergency. *And* if the security guard hadn't been right there taking down the man as he raised his knife to have another crack at the doctor who wasn't doing anything to fix his broken toe.

Aye. There were always egotists in emergency departments demanding they be seen to before anyone else, no matter where the triage nurse put them on the list of waiting patients. What a night that had been. One that wasn't going away any time soon. He'd barely slept since. Every time his eyes closed, a picture appeared in full colour of that knife arcing into him and showing the hatred in his attacker's eyes being replaced with glee when Aaron dropped to the floor in agony. No, sleep was highly overrated when it was full of images he'd give almost anything to forget.

A decent meal would go a long way to quietening the tension that rolled through him on a regular basis for no apparent reason other than he was exhausted and unable to put the attack behind him. A full night's sleep would be even better but not as easy to order up… *No*, make that impossible to order up!

After a quick stop at his house he'd headed to the restaurant he'd seen in town. As he walked in the sound of laughter reached him and he glanced around to see a large table by the far wall with what appeared to be a family having dinner.

His breath caught. Amongst the group sat Bella. And man, was she attractive when she was smiling freely. His gut clenched. He breathed deep and long, urging the tightness to back off. He'd known plenty of beautiful women yet this one seemed to flick a switch, tipping his carefully held-in emotions off balance.

'You'd like a table for one, *signor*?'

He'd far prefer to join Bella's group, but that wasn't happening. Something he should be grateful for. '*Sì.* Thank you.'

'Over here by the window. Not that you can see the lake now that it's dark.' The waitress laughed over her shoulder, her large eyes giving him the once-over. 'But it's a nice place to sit. Away from the noisy family too.'

The family looked right at home. The children were laughing and eating and getting the occasional growl from one of the adults. 'Is this their restaurant?'

'*Sì.* Gino and his wife own it, and the others are all relatives. They eat here most nights of the week.'

Bella appeared to be part of a large family by the looks of that table. A happy family with no restraints on their voices and laughter. Lucky woman. Not something he was used to. Taking the chair the waitress pulled out, he sat down. 'Could I have a glass of Pinot Grigio, please?'

'Certainly. Here's the menu. Tonight's special is the seafood spaghetti.'

Leaning back in his chair, he stared out of the window, aiming for peace and quiet, trying to ignore the unexpected longing bubbling up in him to be involved in such a display of closeness. Beyond the gardens surrounding the parking area, the road was quieter than it had been as he'd made his way to his accommodation after the accident. He'd rented a small house on the hillside overlooking Lake Maggiore for four months, and it was perfect. The views were amazing and the neighbours welcoming without being pushy.

Of course, they knew nothing about him, something he aimed for every time he went somewhere new. Being part of a famous family had drawbacks. He preferred to live quietly and get on with his own career without those of his parents and sister dragging him into media frenzies he disliked intensely. They took away his privacy and his individuality.

Despite the night view, he could see beyond the road to the bumpy lake surface glittering in the light of the full moon peeking over the Alps. The tiny island Isola Bella with its castle was dark except for a few lights on the lower floor. He couldn't have chosen a better place to take a break. The emergency department kept him busy in a more relaxed way than what he was used to. Which meant he wasn't continuously feeling uptight and frantic to keep the patients moving through the system, and not eyeing every one of them as a potential threat. Something else that was a hangover from the attack.

'Here you go, *signor.*' A glass of wine appeared in front of him.

After a quick perusal of the menu he ordered the linguine he'd been looking forward to and sipped the wine. Aye, not a bad way to end a day. Reflected in the window to his right was a view of the family on the other side of the wide room. Even sitting side on to him, Bella stood out. Appearing relaxed and happy, she was talking to the older woman next to her between mouthfuls of pasta. It was as if there were two Bella Rossos. He'd probably only get to know the serious version since they'd mostly see each other at the hospital and even then only when a child was in need of a paediatrician.

With a pang of disappointment he sipped his wine again. At least that was reliable, tasted the same as the first mouthful and wouldn't change by the end of the glass.

It was crazy he should be thinking he'd like to get Bella's attention when he spent most of his time avoiding being noticed. Growing up in his family came with its downside. Because his mother was an actress with multiple awards to her name and his father a top judge often causing a stir in court in London, everyone from the media to hangers-on thought they had a right to know what he was up to and who with any time they asked. As if it had anything to do with them. His sister soaked up the attention like a sponge as she made her way up the ladder as a camerawoman in the movie industry. Not him.

He'd always felt uncomfortable but it had got a whole lot worse when Amy came into his life. That was when he truly grappled with the consequences of his family's fame. In the end Amy left him because she loathed the constant pressure from the media.

Aaron sat back as the waitress placed a plate of linguine in front of him. *'Grazie.'*

Amy had taught him the biggest lesson of his life. Not to judge people until he knew the facts. He'd thought she'd be able to handle being with him because she was quite laid-back and easy-going. He was clearly wrong, or she'd still be with him. Hence his dislike of the media had grown. All he wanted was to be able to get on with his work and personal life without interference, and to help others along the way, whether medically, financially or by lending an ear. One thing he was grateful for at the moment was that it appeared Dr Rosso hadn't recognised his face or name. Then again, here in Stresa there was less likelihood of that happening, which was why he'd applied for the job here.

So relax, why don't you? Make the most of where you are and what you've got. Stop worrying about what you can't change.

Not something he was good at, but he'd give

it a go. For the millionth time. Otherwise coming here was a waste of time. He had to get over the attack so the nightmares stopped, so that he didn't get wound up whenever a patient raised their voice. Only then would life be so much easier to deal with.

The first mouthful of linguine slid across his tongue, exciting his taste buds. 'Delicious.'

'Isn't it?' agreed the waitress as she went past with three full plates balanced on her arm. The smile she gave him was open and suggested she was willing to share something else if he asked.

He smiled to himself. It would be nice to lose himself in a woman for an hour or two, but somehow he couldn't find the enthusiasm to do anything about it.

Sorry, but not tonight, if at all.

Tucking into his meal, he let the food, wine and general atmosphere take over dulling the permanent tension in his body for a while. Something easier to do tonight than he'd experienced in a long time. Nothing to do with Dr Rosso. Couldn't be. He hadn't glanced her way since ordering his meal, and he was trying hard to ignore the image in the window where Bella was now standing and gathering empty plates.

She turned and stopped, her gaze fixed on him. Of course she wouldn't know he could see her in the window. That could be called creepy. He focused on the view once more and forked up another mouthful of pasta. Breathed deep to find that relaxed feeling again. Sipped his wine. Ate some more. Working together was going to be tricky if this was how he reacted to Bella's image in the window.

'Can I get you another wine?' The waitress appeared on the opposite side of his small table. 'Or the dessert menu?'

He leaned back in his chair. 'I'll have a coffee, thank you.'

'Are you staying in Stresa long?' she asked as she took his plate. 'The tourist season is getting under way but already the number of diners at the restaurant is picking up.'

'Is accommodation a part of this business as well?' he asked, avoiding her question. Lights had been on in lots of rooms on the floor above the restaurant when he'd arrived. The car park was also full.

'Level two has eight hotel rooms. Then the

top level is for Gino's family, along with a small apartment where his sister lives. She's having a baby and her brother likes to keep a protective eye on her.' This woman obviously had no inhibitions over talking about the people she worked for.

Best to keep well clear of her, even for a few hours. He knew where a loose tongue could lead and he didn't need that. No one did. 'Coffee?'

Her mouth flattened a little. *'Sì, signor.'*

'Grazie.'

Looking around the room, he noted he was the only one dining alone. Every table had people laughing and talking loudly. Holidaymakers or locals? Most likely a mix as the tourist season was getting up to speed with June being warm while not overly hot.

Coffee finished, Aaron stood up with the intention of paying his tab and heading out into the night. He'd take the car back to his accommodation then go for a stroll beside the lake. A glance across to the family table and he found Bella watching him. Changing direction, he headed her way. It would be rude to walk out without acknowledging her. ‘Hello, Bella. I didn’t expect to see you again so soon.’

‘Aaron, welcome to the family restaurant. I hope you enjoyed your meal.’

A man sitting further along the table stiffened.

‘The linguine was superb,’ Aaron said. ‘I’ll be back to try some of the other dishes during my time in Stresa,’ he added with a smile.

‘You can relax, Gino,’ Bella said. ‘So, Aaron, have you heard how those boys are doing?’

‘Mattia’s had his leg put in a cast and is staying overnight in the hospital. While Andrea has been transferred to the main hospital in Milan where an orthopaedic surgeon will insert a rod in his femur tomorrow.’ He’d called the ED to find out the outcome of the boys’ X-rays before coming here. ‘He’ll be returned to us either tomorrow or the day after.’

‘Bella’s been telling us about the accident. You were there?’ the man he presumed was Gino asked.

‘Yes. I’m Aaron Marshall, working in the ED department over summer.’ He held his hand out to the man.

'Gino Rosso, Bella's brother.' The man had stood up, back straight, a direct look at Aaron.

Your sister's safe with me, pal.

He wasn't interested in getting serious with any woman, not even a beautiful lady with eyes he could drown in. It would only lead to someone being hurt. But Bella was stunningly hot.

'Pleased to meet you. And yes, I reiterate, dinner was delicious.'

'*Grazie.* Do come again.'

Turning back to Bella, Aaron asked, 'How's your side where you took that blow from the woman's elbow?'

'What? Who hit you?' Gino snapped. 'Are you hurt? Bella, answer me.'

After glaring at Aaron, Bella faced off her brother. 'Calm down, Gino. It's nothing. The woman who drove into the boys on the cycle knocked into me when she rushed to check on them. I fell over, that's all.'

Not quite how it happened, but Aaron gave a mental shrug. She'd taken hard knocks in her side and shoulder, and he'd seen her rubbing where she'd been hit a couple of times at the accident scene. But if Bella didn't want her brother getting wound up by the fact that it had been a deliberate knock, then he'd go along with her. He had to work with this woman, and any hindrance could be a pain in the backside. 'It was a little chaotic for a few moments, but the woman was removed and we got on with helping the boys.'

Gino eyeballed him, then nodded. 'Thank you for being there for Bella.'

He'd have done the same thing for anyone. 'No problem.'

'I'd better get back to the kitchen. Those cooks are slack when I'm not there to watch over them.'

Bella shook her head at her brother. 'They're too scared of you to take a breath.' Her voice was full of affection. 'He only talks tough. He's a pussycat on the inside.'

Gino strode away without comment.

'Whichever, he's a darned good chef. People say pasta's pasta, how can you go wrong with cooking it? I disagree. Done well, nothing beats it.'

'You're from Scotland?'

'Yes. Our food couldn't be more different.'

'I lived in London for four years and hankered after Gino's cooking all the time.'

Glancing around to make sure none of the family was within hearing, he found he was being sized up by the older woman Bella had been sitting by.

Wasting your time, lady.

The other man still remaining resembled Gino, and Bella, he saw now he looked more closely. Another brother, most like. He turned back to Bella and said quietly, 'Are you sure you're all right? She did slam into you fairly hard.'

'I'm fine. Thank you for asking though. Now I'd better get the table cleared. I'll see you at the hospital tomorrow or later on in the week. Goodnight.' She added more dirty plates to those she already held and walked away.

'Goodnight, Bella.'

She didn't look back.

Fair enough. Though it was a new experience for him. It was usually he who drew the line under getting too friendly. He headed to the young man standing at the desk. 'I'd like to pay my bill, thank you.'

'It's been taken care of, sir. Gino said the meal was on him.'

'That can't be right. I only met him a few minutes ago.'

'You looked out for Bella today. That means a lot to this family. Goodnight, sir. Hopefully we'll see you again some time soon.'

Stunned, Aaron wandered outside. He couldn't remember ever being thanked in that way. People usually wanted something from him. Even though this family didn't know who he was, he doubted it would've made a difference if they did. He liked that a lot.

But a meal on the house? For helping Bella to her feet? Any decent man would have done the same.

Hold on. The waitress mentioned a sister living upstairs. A pregnant sister. Bella? That would explain the concern in her eyes as she rubbed her side. He hadn't noticed her being pregnant but then he hadn't been looking hard. If she was pregnant then she was out of bounds. There was already a man in her life.

Hard to explain the disappointment filling him as he walked out to his car though.

CHAPTER TWO

'BELLA, PHONE FOR YOU. It's ED.' Gita handed the phone over.

'Bella Rosso speaking.'

'Bella, it's Aaron. We've got a fourteen-year-old girl presenting with injuries after a fall. But I think there's something else going on that might've caused her to trip in the first place. Can you come along to see her?' He sounded professional, nothing like the sexy man she'd met three days ago.

Which was good since they'd be working together, and because she wasn't interested in him anyway, sexy or not.

Sure, Bella.

So why hadn't she been able to put him out of her mind ever since she'd first bumped into him at the accident, even when she had more important things to think about? 'On my way.'

'Thanks.' *Click.* He'd gone.

Not sticking around to talk about anything

else, then. She should be thankful, given some of the locum doctors thought chatting about anything *but* their patient was fine. But she couldn't help but feel a little disgruntled. Hadn't he wanted to say hello? Or ask why she didn't want Gino knowing how that woman had flattened her so easily?

She'd seen the look on his face when she'd downplayed the altercation. He'd clearly taken note of her reluctance to alarm Gino. Her brother fussed over her enough without adding to it with a minor thing that had no repercussions. 'I'm heading to ED,' she told Nurse Gita. 'Here's a new prescription for Joseph. I'm not happy with how the infection's taking so long to clear so he's to stay in for another night. We'll get some more bloods done too.'

Joseph had a high white cell count with abundant immature neutrophils, backing the diagnosis of infection in his abdomen where he'd had an appendectomy three days ago. She hadn't done the surgery, but had been left with the problem of clearing his infection. Now she was beginning to think there was more going on than just an infection.

She signed the lab form she'd printed off.

'There you go. Haematology and biochemistry samples.' Standing up, she rubbed the dull ache remaining in her side where that woman's elbow had got her. Better remember not to do that in front of Dr Aaron. He'd be quick to comment, and she already had enough people keeping a beady eye on her.

Anyone would think she was incapable of looking out for herself. So untrue. She'd managed perfectly well since Jason's illness and passing, thank you very much. Sort of, anyway. Lonely at times, and at first it'd been hard to make decisions about her future, but these days she was back on her feet and coping just fine. She'd also made a big decision and it was nestled inside her, keeping safe. Her hand slid to her growing abdomen, touched lightly. 'Hey, baby, how're you doing?'

'You all right?' Gita asked.

Damn it. She really needed to be circumspect on where and when she talked to her baby. 'I'm fine,' she said firmly. Then with a long sigh, 'Sorry, Gita. I didn't mean to snap. I had a bit of a sleepless night, that's all.' It was true. Dreams of Jason had got mixed up with images of a tall Scotsman looking out for her at the accident scene and then kept her awake for hours trying to forget them.

'I had lots of those during both my pregnancies. Worrying about everything under the sun.'

'Glad to know I'm normal, then.' She laughed tightly as she headed out of the door. Nothing normal about thinking of another man when she was carrying her late husband's child. *Or was it?* Who knew what was normal any more? Her world had been tipped upside down and sent spinning out of control when Jason was diagnosed with end-stage myeloma. She might be back on track, but there were days—and nights—when she really wondered if she was plain nuts to be having a baby on her own even when they'd discussed it in depth time and again in the final weeks of Jason's life. Talk was one thing, reality quite another.

It was strange not having Jason around to share the excitement and talk about baby's future with. He'd been happy for her to have their child, but it wasn't the same as him actually being here with her. She'd known what she was letting herself in for before undergoing the IVF—or so she'd thought. Some days it was a little scary thinking about what lay ahead, but mostly it was exciting.

'Morning, Bella.' Aaron crossed the emergency room when she walked in. Aaron's dark blue eyes were locked on her, sending an unexpected shiver down her spine. 'How's things?'

'All good, thanks.'

Apart from this sense of awakening that's developed since I laid eyes on you.

What was wrong with her? Even if she opened up to the possibility, there was no room for romance in her life with baby on the way.

'Glad to hear that.' He took a quick step back. Too close?

'Tell me more about your young patient.' She needed to focus on work, and ignore the odd sensations Aaron was causing. Odd in that she hadn't felt anything close to desire in years. Also totally out of place. Getting into a long-term relationship now she was carrying her and Jason's baby would be awkward. He'd never get the opportunity to meet his child, and to bring another man into the picture mightn't work. Anyway, she intended to raise it herself.

Don't say that to your brothers.

They were already getting their digs in about how to bring up him or her.

'Tish Gambolli presented with a fractured wrist and concussion after falling off a first-floor deck. There's a rash on her face and swelling in her arms. Her mother says the swelling and rash have been apparent for a couple of months but became worse over the last couple of days.' Aaron led the way to a computer and brought up the notes he'd entered.

'Is Tish a local?' If so there might be info from earlier medical incidents.

'The family's visiting from Genoa for a month, staying with relatives.'

Nothing to go by then. Leaning closer to read the brief notes pertaining to Tish, Bella tried to ignore the pervading scent of the outdoors emanating from the man beside her. Hard to do when he was so close. The smell brought back old memories of walking in the hills beyond the town with Jason the first time he came here to meet her family. How did this guy get that scent? It didn't come in an aerosol can. Had he been out walking in the early hours that morning? He might be someone who leapt out of bed when the sun peeked over the horizon and got outdoors to make the most of the day before it became too hot.

Talking about hot, there was a wave of heat blasting through her right now and it had nothing to do with her physical condition. Stepping sideways, she said, 'Take me to meet her.'

'Sure,' he drawled in that sexy accent.

'Sorry, I didn't mean to be so abrupt.' That was what happened when she needed to dampen down the sudden awareness of him.

'No problem. I told Tish's mother I was seeking your opinion. She's happy with that.'

'Good.'

'Along here.' Aaron led her past a row of unoccupied cubicles to the end of the room, where he swished back the curtain and indicated she should enter first. 'Tish, this is Dr Rosso,' he said over her shoulder, startling her. Damn, she was edgy around him.

'*Ciao*, Tish. Call me Bella.'

'My head hurts.' Her speech was slurred, no doubt due to the concussion Aaron mentioned.

'I'm sure Aaron has that under control.'

'I've administered mild analgesics,' Aaron told her. 'This is Gabby, Tish's mother.'

'Hello, Gabby. I hear Tish hasn't been feeling well lately, with rashes and some swelling happening.' The teen's face was red with a rash around her eyes. Aaron was on the ball with this one. He probably was with all his patients. He had that air of confidence about him that would lead patients to believe in him.

'That's correct.'

Why hadn't they been to a doctor about this? 'Tish, can I look at your arms?'

Tish nodded. 'All right.'

'Tell me if it hurts when I touch you.' The limbs were hot and spongy where Bella prodded carefully.

Tish didn't complain about any pain, which was a plus.

'I need you to sit up so I can look at your head.' Bella knew hair loss could be a side effect of lupus.

Tish shuffled up the bed, then swayed and fell sideways, her eyes staring sightlessly.

Aaron was immediately at her side, catching her before she slid over the edge of the bed. 'Easy does it.'

'What happened?' shrieked Tish's mother.

'She fainted,' Bella answered as she helped Aaron move the girl to the centre of the bed.

What was going on? 'Concussion, then a faint.' Bella's finger was on Tish's pulse. 'Erratic.'

Tish's eyes opened. 'Mamma?'

'I'm here, sweetheart.'

'I feel sick.'

Aaron had a bowl out of the bedside cabinet and next to Tish before she'd finished talking. 'Use this if necessary.'

Bella gave her a few minutes then asked, 'I need to find out Tish's haemoglobin level. Do you get overly tired at times, Tish?'

'Sometimes,' she muttered reluctantly.

'Most days,' Gabby intervened. 'I thought that was due to her age and her body changing from a girl to a woman.'

Tish blushed and looked anywhere but at Aaron, who discreetly turned away to study the monitor by the bed.

Points for his empathy, Bella thought. Not a pushy male doctor who believed all female patients should accept his presence because he *was* a doctor.

There was quite a bit to like about him.

As in working comfortably alongside him when necessary, nothing else.

Right.

He was hard to ignore though.

'I'll arrange for some bloods to be taken and sent off to the lab.'

She had barely finished her sentence when a nurse appeared at the door. 'Aaron, the ambulance has arrived with two tourists who went over the side of the hill on cycles. One with serious injuries. Luka wants all hands on deck. He's already tied up with a cardio infarct.'

'Coming.'

'Need my help?' Bella asked, sensing the urgency in his voice.

'Sounds like it,' Aaron answered, already heading out of the cubicle. Then he spun back around. 'Tish, Gabby, we'll be back as soon as possible. In the meantime take it easy. One of the nurses will keep an eye on you. There's nothing to panic about.'

As Bella scrubbed up next to Aaron she couldn't help thinking how they were about to work together in an emergency for the second time in only a few days. It was rare for her to be helping in ED other than when it was a child specifically referred to her for specialist treatment. It was as though some outside force was saying, *You two are meant to be together.*

But they weren't.

Aaron made her toes tingle with just one look, but that was not a reason to get serious about him.

In medical situations he made everything look so easy. Was he like that outside the hospital walls? Or was this merely his professional manner and he was more demanding of people in his personal life?

He hadn't been the other night at the restaurant.

Instead he was quiet and appreciative of his dinner. He didn't pester her about how she felt after being knocked over earlier once he understood Gino would get concerned. It didn't necessarily mean a lot. Aaron might've been on his best behaviour, though somehow she found that hard to believe. Everything she'd observed about him so far said he was a good guy who thought about others, the kind of man she went for. If she was going for one, which she wasn't.

She'd had the love of her life, and no one got a second crack at that. Not often anyway, and chances were she wouldn't. Taking another chance on love didn't feel right. She'd been so lucky with Jason. Now she was following up by having his baby. Her family had backed her all the way once Jason talked to them about it, as he did with his parents. They too accepted her decision to go through with motherhood, but she doubted they'd be so happy if she found a new man to live with, and thereby become the father of their son's child. After three years they were still clinging to Jason, almost as if he'd stepped out for a few hours and would be home any moment.

Entering the ED drew her attention back to the intense situation. A stretcher was being wheeled into the department, the young man lying on it attached to fluids and a breathing apparatus. A cervical collar held his head still. The paramedic handed Aaron a clipboard. 'Jonathon Stitchbury, twenty-four. He took full impact on the head when he went over the side of the hill on his bike, has no reaction in his feet to touch. He's been unconscious all the time we've been with him, and the people who found him say he was like that all the time. He also has deep lacerations to his lower back, shoulders and upper arms.'

'Thanks.' Aaron was reading the notes.

'Emano, tell Luka I need Bella with me on this one. He might need to call in someone else.'

The hospital was small and not set up to cater for a huge influx of patients or more than a couple requiring urgent attention and equipment, so in major emergency crises doctors from all the departments were available to help in ED.

'He's already onto it,' the nurse replied as he made ready with the spinal board for them to shift Jonathon across to the hospital bed.

Bella took her place at one corner. It had been a long time since she'd helped a patient with a serious spinal injury but she hadn't forgotten the tension amongst the medical staff as they raced to save the person from further problems all the while hoping against the odds that there'd be nothing too wrong.

'One, two, three,' Emano said, and he and the paramedic rolled Jonathon onto his side so Bella and Aaron could slide a board under him to lower his body down without inflicting more damage.

'Bella, you start at the feet while I check his abdomen and chest.' Aaron was already cutting the sports pants away to expose Jonathon's lower body.

'Onto it.' Definitely no response to the tapping and prodding on the man's feet. She lifted a hand and tapped the palm. The patient's fingers curled instinctively. Same result with the other hand. 'Feeling in both arms.'

'Internal injuries are likely given the impact he's obviously undergone.' Aaron's fingers were pressing gently around the abdomen, but there was an urgency about him that made her wonder if he'd already found an injury.

Placing the stethoscope on Jonathon's chest, she listened to the heartbeat. It was slow and erratic. Then…silence. 'Code one,' she snapped and clasped her hands together to begin compressions. 'One, two, three, four.' Continuing to push and release, she willed the young man to live.

Aaron stepped up, ready to breathe into the man's lungs when she reached thirty compressions. 'He's bleeding internally. Majorly, I'd say.'

Emano shoved the defibrillator into his hands.

Within seconds Aaron had the pads in place

and was waiting impatiently for the machine to get up to speed. Moments later the alarm sounded and he said, 'Stand back, everyone.' After looking to make certain no one stood close enough to get an electrical zap, he pressed the button.

Jonathon's body jerked upward, fell back. The flat line on the screen began rising and falling.

Bella felt her heart begin pounding as she placed the stethoscope back in place on the man's chest. 'That was close.'

'I don't think we're out of trouble yet,' Aaron said. He looked around. 'Emano, get ready for a procedure. Bella, call the duty anaesthetist, though I can't wait if he's not in the hospital. I'm going in asap. I need to stop the blood loss before another cardiac arrest occurs.'

Bella raced to the phone on the wall and pressed the theatre number. It might be a small hospital but they had staff to cover most emergencies. She got a voice message and left one of her own just in case the anaesthetist got it in time. 'Jack, you're needed in ED. Now.' Slamming the phone down, she returned to Jonathon's side and took over listening to his heart and monitoring his obs so Aaron could prep for the incision he had to make. 'No one picked up.'

'Probably in Theatre,' Aaron acknowledged, his face grim. 'We have to do this.'

'Tell me what you want all the way,' Bella said, aware of every move he made and the tension growing in his shoulders. He was on high alert. Did he think his patient was going to bleed out before he repaired the injury? It was possible. Nearly an hour had passed since the man fell off the cliffside. 'You've got this, Aaron,' she said quietly.

'You don't know that yet.' He was inside the abdomen feeling for the bleeding site. 'Got it. Emano, suture kit. Bella, press here hard.' He took her hand and placed it where his had been. Sweat was breaking out on his forehead. Something was up with him. It was possible he'd lost a patient before in a similar crisis, and doctors never forget those experiences, questioning themselves over whether they could have done something more to save the person.

The heart monitor alarmed again.

Bella kept her hand in place until the last possible moment, stepped back while the shock was delivered, then returned to put pressure back on the bleeding site. 'At least his heart started again,' she said, more to herself than anyone else.

'One thing to be grateful for,' Aaron answered as he began suturing the torn blood vessel between Bella's fingers. *If this man doesn't survive I'm going to kick myself for ever and beyond*, he thought as he pulled the thread through and tied it off. His colleagues had done this for him the night he was attacked and they'd told him how hard it was with him being a mate and fellow doctor. He mightn't know Jonathon but the pressure to get this right even when he was on the back foot with it being so long since the injury happened was driving him hard.

Bella shifted her hand slightly to allow him to place the next suture. She had her eye on the job. Certainly knew what she was doing.

'Next needle,' he demanded.

Emano passed one over, took the other out of the way.

The needle went through, and he tied another knot. Nearly there. He held his hand out for another needle.

Bella leaned closer, said quietly, 'Breathe.'

He hadn't realised he wasn't. Inhale, exhale. Put another stitch in place. Inhale. Now Bella would have questions he had no intention of answering. Too bad. The bleeding was slowing as the hole became tiny. Almost there. He was winning. That was all that mattered. That and ordering O-negative blood for Jonathon. Damn, he should've done something about that already. As if there'd been time. 'Bella, can you call the lab for some blood?' He didn't need her pressure on the wound now.

'On it.'

He liked how she didn't muck around, just did whatever he asked. No ego in sight. This was his domain but over the years in emergency departments he had come across one or two specialists wanting to flex a muscle just to show they knew their job. 'Thanks.'

He doubted she heard him; she was only focused on what was important as she lifted the phone. They worked well together in emergencies. He'd laugh if it weren't ridiculous. They worked in different medical fields and for this to happen twice in a few days was weird. It was as if they were meant to get to know each other.

There, last suture done. He straightened up and stood back to look Jonathon over. His skin was white, his breathing laboured—but at least he was breathing with the aid of the oxygen pump. His heart rate was slow but stable. Aaron sighed with relief. He'd done it. They'd done it. Bella, Emano and him. This was one patient he wasn't going to spend weeks wondering if he could've done more for. There was still a lot to do, like getting blood into his patient, and preparing him for the journey to a hospital in Milan, but the odds were on Jonathon's side now.

'Here. For your face.' Bella was back, handing him a wipe. She must have noticed his moist brow. Then she went back to the monitors, studying them intently as though trying to give him some space.

Guess she'd seen another side to him. He *had* stressed, but nothing serious enough to get in the way of making certain his patient survived. He rubbed the sweat off his brow and face and tossed the wipe in the bin.

'You were a great help.' Very calm and logical. Beautiful came to mind. Beautiful in how she worked. Not once had she tensed or looked flustered. She'd got on with doing what needed to be done and did it competently, never questioning him. He gasped. When she'd told him to breathe *he* had calmed down and got a grip on his emotions. That attack in Edinburgh had a lot to answer for. He'd always wanted the best outcome for any patient, but since that horrific night he felt more in touch with what someone like Jonathon had just gone through. His actions weren't impeded, but his body reacted with tension—*and faulty breathing, apparently*.

Bella flicked him a brief smile. 'If you don't need me for anything else, I'll get back to Tish. I have some patient appointments to get back to at the clinic.'

The department would feel empty without her. 'We've got this now. Again, thanks for your assistance.'

'You're overdoing it.' She grinned.

And just like that, his stomach tightened and his head spun. Bella Rosso was something else. Something, no, *someone* he didn't need in his life right now. Somehow he didn't think that was going to change a thing. She was already nudging her way in without even trying. If she really turned her attention on him, he didn't stand a chance. He had to get real here. 'That's me. An over-doer.'

Two hours later Bella was back in the department, and his heart was beating faster than normal, telling him he needed to work at sorting his act out, because she was getting to him without any effort. The problem was he couldn't avoid her around the hospital. Nor did he really want to, if he was being honest with himself. 'Have you got some results back on Tish?' he asked.

Her nod was abrupt. 'I have.'

'Not good?'

'I'm certain about the lupus. Well spotted,' she added with a grim look.

'I was hoping I'd got it wrong, but the hair loss was a give away.'

'I know that feeling,' she said. 'I'll arrange for her to go to the children's ward for the night so we can get started on some treatment. I'd like her to get a good night's sleep too.'

Sleep. What was that? Suddenly Aaron yawned. It had been a big day and wasn't over yet. Dinner at Gino's *ristorante* was starting to look like a good idea. It was nearby and had a relaxed atmosphere, something he needed right now. All he'd have to do was turn up, sit down and enjoy the wonderful food.

Bella looked his way. 'Late night?'

'No, more of a restless night than any other night. Too much going on in my head.'

'I hate those nights.'

I hope your nights aren't as bad as mine, Aaron thought. Pictures of a knife-wielding man were not easy to get over, if at all. Sometimes he wondered if the nightmares would ever go away entirely, or if he had to accept this was his new normal. 'They're not much fun,' he said. 'Those results came back quickly.' The downside to being some distance from the city and the medical laboratories was how long it took to get tests done. Glancing down, he noticed her hand stroking her abdomen.

Did she realise she was rubbing her lower belly as she walked? He stilled. As in how pregnant women touched their stomach sometimes. So Bella *was* the sister living in the building where the restaurant was. So much for getting in a twist over her. She was already taken. Now he thought about it, her first reaction when that woman sent her sprawling on the ground was to touch her belly as she was doing now. He could be wrong, but his gut said not. Bella Rosso was pregnant and looking radiant. And unavailable for a quick fling, which was all he could give her right now. Not that he'd ever suggest it, but he had been thinking about it ever since they met. It was hard not to when she oozed sexiness.

There again, she always held herself back around him, making certain they were only on a professional footing. Even when he'd spoken to her at the restaurant she hadn't been overly friendly towards him. Now he knew she had a partner he could shut down the annoying pull that gripped him whenever she was near. Maybe not a husband though as there was no sign of a wedding ring, and she hadn't been with a man at dinner. Of course, the guy might be away for work or anything.

Stop trying to fill in all the gaps when you've got nothing to go on.

With a sigh he hated to admit was filled with regret, he got busy so he could stop thinking about one beautiful, confident doctor. Until the next time she came into the department, and he'd have to start over. She really was mucking with his head, and that was so unusual it was odd, and interesting. He liked Bella. Furthermore, he wanted to spend time with her and get to know her better. But the last thing she needed was him complicating matters for her.

'Want to come with me to tell Tish and Gabby?'

All right, she could surprise him. 'Since it's quiet in here now, yes.'

'Good answer.' She suddenly smiled.

His head spun a little. That smile should be bottled for bad days. 'Let's go,' he growled around the lump of longing forming in the back of his throat.

'Here they come,' Tish said in a worry-laden voice as they approached her bed. 'Good or bad news?' There was a brave smile on her pale face but her eyes were flitting everywhere.

As they entered the cubicle, Bella pulled up a chair and sat down looking at her notes. 'Tish, you do have lupus. The good news is that it's very mild and we need to focus on keeping it that way.'

'Can't you give me something to make it go away?'

Gabby reached for her daughter's hand and held it tight. 'Tell us more, Doctor. Is Tish going to be all right?'

'Yes, she is, but not quite as she knows things now. Tish, you'll probably have to take regular medications to keep your thyroid under control and that might interfere with your energy levels at times.' She was putting it mildly for now, aiming for a calm approach. The specialist Tish would see would dig deeper and let the family know more as he progressed. It wasn't her place to start going into what lay ahead.

'Do we have to go back to Genoa to see a specialist right now?' Tish asked in a quiet voice.

'I doubt it. I'm sending your notes through to a clinic today but, as we all know, getting an appointment with a specialist takes time. You can carry on enjoying your holiday with your cousins in the meantime. Just keep that cast out of the water while you're at it.' Bella stood up and gave Tish and Gabby a big smile. 'Have some fun, and try not to worry too much.'

'Easy for you to say.'

'Tish, that's not nice,' Gabby admonished her daughter.

Bella paused. 'Tish, I hear you. You have a lot to deal with and there will be days you'll struggle, but you're strong so I believe you'll do all right.'

Aaron blinked. Never had he heard a specialist be so honest with a young patient. 'Tish, Gabby, I told you Dr Rosso was good, didn't I?'

Tish was crying. 'Sorry, Bella.'

'It's fine. Trust me, you *will* cope.' She drew a breath. 'Tish, I want you to stay in hospital overnight so I can start you on some drugs to help lift your energy levels.'

'Do I have to?'

'Yes. I'll be in early tomorrow to check you over, then if everything's going well you can get on with enjoying your holiday, though at a slower pace. All right?'

'I suppose so.'

Gabby wiped a stray tear away. 'Thank you, Doctor. I'm so glad we met you.'

'If you've got any more questions, fire away. I'll give you my number because you're bound to think of something later on.'

When Bella left the cubicle Aaron could feel

his heart pounding. She was special. Not only as a doctor. If she could be so understanding with her patient, then she'd be the same with everyone. Her baby was going to be one lucky individual having her for a mother.

Why did she have to be pregnant with another man's baby?

He would like nothing more than to get to know every part of her.

Thank goodness she was pregnant, then, because he wasn't ready to fall in love again. The last time had been a heartbreaker. Amy had been a nurse at the hospital in New Zealand where he was doing a post-grad year and he'd been smitten from the moment he met her in the emergency department. They'd moved in together within four months and everything was perfect. When he proposed and Amy said yes, he truly believed nothing could go wrong in his world. Except being on the other side of the globe, living a quiet life, he'd been letting his guard down over how the media would get into a frenzy when the news got out. Which was exactly what happened when his parents announced their son was getting married upon his return to Britain over the summer.

All hell broke loose. At first Amy coped with the drama and fame and being followed everywhere. She refused to be intimidated but at the same time preferred to remain in the background, making him relieved and so proud of her. She also supported him and became a part of his life in England. Then she grew quieter and less communicative. He tried to get her to tell him what was wrong, but she'd shrug away his questions. One night he came home from a harrowing day in the emergency department to find a letter on the table and one half of the wardrobe empty. Amy had gone. She couldn't handle the lifestyle that went with the Marshall clan and had gone back to New Zealand.

He followed her in an attempt to win her back but she refused to give him a chance, saying she could not live with all that 'uncalled-for attention' for another day. Heartbroken, he flew home, swearing he'd never again hand over his heart so readily, if at all. Six months later he heard she'd married her childhood sweetheart. So much for loving him if she could do an about-face so fast. The lesson for him was that love came with a huge price tag he wasn't prepared to pay.

Which meant he'd better find somewhere else to have dinner tonight. The less time spent in Bella's space, the better. She was too attractive to ignore, too tempting, so putting distance between them whenever possible was the only way to go.

CHAPTER THREE

JUST AFTER SIX Aaron was ready to head out of the department. The late afternoon had turned busy with a car versus truck ending with two seriously injured men being brought in, and then a three-year-old with a dog bite arrived with her mother freaking out. Add in the usual cases of suspected broken bones and a woman with severe abdominal pains and he hadn't been able to walk off duty at three when everyone was struggling to deal with the influx. It had been the busiest day he'd had in this ED. Still a lot quieter than back in Edinburgh. 'That's it. I'm heading away while I can.'

'Thanks for staying back to help us,' Tommaso said.

'No problem.'

'Where is she? Why can't I take her home?' a man shouted from behind him.

Looking around, Aaron saw an older man charging through the department, a look of pure rage darkening his craggy face. Aaron's gut squeezed. There wasn't a knife in the fist the man waved at a nurse, but still, he could feel the anxious energy in his body building. 'Here we go again.' His stomach tightened painfully as he started towards the guy.

Bella appeared at the other end of the row of cubicles. 'Hello. Can I help you?' she asked the man.

'Step away, Bella,' Aaron said calmly so as not to disturb the guy any further, but he was going to intervene before anyone got hurt. Especially Bella. Stepping between her and the angry man, he stood straight and tall. 'Stop shouting and talk to me. I'm a doctor. Who do you want to see?'

'What's it to you? Think you can stop me, huh?'

I'll do my best.

'Slow down and talk to me,' he repeated. 'Unless you do, I won't know what your problem is.'

Knuckles slammed into his chest. 'My wife's been here for hours and no one's looking after her. She's sick, and no one cares.'

Fighting the urge to grab the man and hold

him until security came, Aaron drew a breath and said with as much calm as he could muster, 'What's your wife's name?'

The man spun around and stormed over to a bed where a woman being monitored for heart murmurs lay looking embarrassed. Jabbing the air with his forefinger, he shouted, 'This is her. See? No one's with her. She needs to be looked after.'

The woman had come in alone an hour ago feeling unwell. Given her history of heart problems, she'd been attached to an array of monitors and a nurse had been with her most of the time. Except now.

'Come with me and I'll show you what we're doing to help your wife.'

The man whirled around and pushed his face right up to Aaron's. 'Why should I believe anything you say?'

'Because I have no reason to lie to you.' Thump, thump, went his heart. He doubted he was about to get attacked, but the day he was stabbed he hadn't seen the knife coming until it was too late.

'Mrs Romano is being well cared for. Her heart was erratic when she arrived but is returning to normal. We'll continue to monitor her for a while to come. She'll probably go to the ward overnight. Now, if you want to, you can sit with her.'

The man's shoulders sagged as the anger drained away. 'She's had heart attacks before. Nearly died twice.'

The poor man was terrified this might've been the time his wife didn't make it. Aaron relaxed as much as possible. But relaxing didn't come easy for him.

'I understand your worry.' Aaron suddenly realised how quiet the department had become. Looking around, he found everyone, patients, nurses and doctors, watching the unfolding scene. Bella's concern was all over her face. For him, if her focus was anything to go by. His chest expanded. The pounding under his ribs slowed.

He didn't attack, relax.

Bella was coming towards him, compassion in those beautiful green eyes. He put a hand up, embarrassed to see it shaking. 'Wait.' Turning to the patient's husband, he said, 'Can we have your reassurance you won't lose your temper again? Otherwise you will be removed from the department for the safety of other patients and their visitors, and all our staff.'

'I get so stressed every time Ro gets sick.' The man gulped. 'I'm sorry. I won't cause any more trouble.'

Tommaso, a fellow doctor, moved in and, reassuringly taking Mr Romano's arm, led him to a chair beside his wife. 'Sit here, and if you have any questions please wait until a nurse or doctor is available to talk to you.' He looked over his shoulder to Aaron. 'You're amazing. Now go home. See you tomorrow.'

Suddenly Aaron felt so tired he could barely lift his feet. Bella took his arm and gently tugged him away. 'Come on. We'll go outside and get our breath.'

Knowing she'd feel him shaking wasn't enough to make him pull his arm away from her hold. He needed her strength for a moment. It felt good to share his stress, even when she didn't know why he was acting like this. Her fingers were firm yet light and her shoulder brushed his upper arm as they walked out of the department. He couldn't help the lustful heat the subtle touch evoked within him.

Once away from everyone, she dropped her

hand and put a gap between them, as though her gesture wasn't to be seen as anything too personal, clearly taking stock of how seriously he'd reacted. 'When did you last eat?' she asked.

That was unexpected. 'Some time this morning.'

'You're not looking after yourself, Aaron.'

'Now who's sounding like one of her brothers?' he quipped in an attempt to lighten her sombre mood.

'It's a family thing. You haven't heard my mother yet.' She smiled.

'Was she not there the other night?'

'She'd gone upstairs to check on one of the grandkids when you came over. Let's walk a bit to calm down after that altercation and then we'll head home for dinner.'

For someone who always seemed in a hurry to move on from talking to him, she'd just managed to surprise the pants off him. Not literally, thank goodness. 'That's not necessary.' But he'd like time unwinding with her, chilling out and putting the nightmare behind him. Though today's scenario had nothing on what happened last time, it reminded him how easily things could go from normal to terrifying in a blink.

'A meal with my noisy family can't hurt, even if it's not what you're used to,' she said. 'You were very composed dealing with that man. He was beside himself with worry. I don't know how you managed not to get in his face and tell him to get out of the department.'

Nor did he. But then last time he'd been much the same. It was the same every time he was confronted by irate patients or someone with a patient thinking nothing was being done to help them. It must be part of him to remain cool and calm in adverse situations. Usually it worked—*until that last time in Edinburgh.* Though he'd been told he was very calm right up until the knife sliced into him.

'That would've exacerbated the situation.'

'You know that? From experience?' Of course she read him that easily. She was smart.

'Yes.'

Please don't ask any more.

'There's a shortcut to the lake along here. Come on.' She strode out, forcing him to increase his pace.

Not hard to do when he was enjoying being

with her, despite what had happened minutes ago. It helped that she didn't follow up with intense questions he wasn't prepared to answer. 'We're not far from the restaurant, are we?' he noted when they reached the shore of Lake Maggiore.

'Just under a kilometre away.'

'Shall we walk there?'

'Of course. So you will join my family for dinner?' She sounded far more open to him than she had any time previously, making it hard not to accept her invitation. Even knowing he shouldn't be interested in anything about her outside work he couldn't say no. 'They won't mind?'

'Not at all. It's always a bit of a circus at mealtimes but it's how we like it. Happy families.' There was a lot of love in her voice.

Which made him a little jealous. 'When I was growing up my family was always too busy to sit down together at the end of the day and talk about what we'd been up to.' That was when he lived at home and wasn't at boarding school or living in student quarters at university.

'I can't imagine what that's like.' She paused.

'No, that's not true. Jason's parents were a little like that, always rushing in for dinner and rushing off to some meeting or work before they'd swallowed the last mouthful.'

'Jason?'

'My husband.' Bella went quiet on him. Needing space?

He waited for more as they walked along the narrow path towards town.

'He died three years ago.'

The air oozed out of his lungs at the pain in her voice. 'I'm sorry to hear that, Bella. Really sorry.' How did anyone cope with the death of their partner? 'It's not much, but I don't know what else to say.'

'It's enough,' she said through a tight smile. 'Better than saying something meaningless.'

So it wasn't her husband's baby she was carrying? She must've moved on despite that pain he'd heard. All number of questions were firing up in his head but he left her alone, knowing how much he hated people delving into his life. It was something he'd grown up dealing with. People thought they had every right to ask personal questions about his love life, his wealth, his career. About anything really.

He wouldn't do that to her, but he did want to know more.

Ten minutes later they were walking up the road where Bella's family lived. Some of them, anyway.

'How many siblings have you got?'

'Three bossy brothers, three lovely sisters-in-law and five nieces and nephews.' Her hand did that touch-the-tummy thing.

'You're very lucky.' A wave of longing rolled through him. It would be awesome to have his own family but he'd long believed it wouldn't happen. Not since Amy left and he'd decided he wasn't getting involved with anyone again. Having his heart broken was not something he ever wanted to face again. He'd really believed he and Amy were for ever. He'd given his all to their relationship. She'd cut him in half when she walked away. Yet here was Bella making him think about family and love. It didn't make sense.

'You're right, I am.'

He remembered something the waitress had said the other night. 'So you live above the restaurant? Along with your family?'

Her eyebrows rose in an exquisite manner,

making him hum on the inside. 'Someone's been talking. Yes, I have the small one-bedroom apartment on the far side. At some point I'll get a place of my own, but for now the arrangement works well. I get to spend time with my family and Gino makes sure I eat way too much.'

Aaron laughed. 'Now, that doesn't surprise me.' What did though was that Bella was apparently on her own. No mention of a partner at all. Yet she was pregnant. Interesting. It wasn't any of his business but that didn't stop him wanting to know. He wasn't stupid though. Ask about that and he was sure he'd not only miss out on a wonderful meal but he'd be sent to emotional purgatory for the rest of his time in Stresa and working with Bella would become difficult beyond belief.

'Right, brace yourself,' Bella said, and they were inside the restaurant and she was heading to the same table she'd been at the other night where five children sat eating while four adults were talking with wine glasses at hand. 'Come on, Aaron. Time to meet the tribe for a grilling.'

That alone would've normally sent him running for the door, but somehow he didn't think this was going to be too intrusive, and more like fun.

'Mamma, Papà, I'd like you to meet Aaron Marshall. He's a relieving doctor at the emergency centre and is in need of a decent dinner.'

'Welcome.' Bella's father clapped him on the shoulder. 'We like it when Bella brings someone home for a meal.'

That might be tricky. He was only a colleague. 'Thanks for having me.'

Her mother wrapped him in a hug. 'Hello, Aaron. Didn't you dine here earlier in the week?'

'I did, and the food was delicious.'

'I heard that.' Gino appeared from out the back.

'Just as well I didn't say it was awful.'

Gino laughed. 'You'd already be halfway across the deck if you had.'

He didn't doubt it. The man appeared fit and strong, despite a stomach that suggested he sampled his cooking rather a lot. 'I did plan on coming back during the weekend, but when Bella suggested I join you all tonight I couldn't resist.' It was true. He'd seen the love at the table last time he was here and felt envious. To give up an opportunity to join in would be crazy.

Bella intervened. 'We've been very busy at work, and have only just finished. I'm starving and think Aaron might be feeling the same.' She did the introductions of everyone around the table.

'I hope I remember all the names.' He chuckled. 'There's quite a crowd of you.'

Cara, or was it Anna, one of the sisters-in-law, laughed. 'I wanted them all to wear name tags when I first became part of the family. You'll soon know who's who.'

That sounded as though he'd be turning up regularly. 'I hope so.'

Bella pulled out two chairs and sat down on one. 'Here you go, Aaron. Get comfortable before the inquisition starts.'

Really? This family would start tormenting him with questions he hated answering? He hesitated. Bella looked at him and smiled. 'It's all right. I was teasing.'

Her smile went a long way to undoing the knots forming in his belly. It was genuine and, as far as he could see, not laced with an agenda.

He sank further onto the seat before any more doubts crept in. 'So far I haven't known you to be so light-hearted.'

'There's a lot you don't know about me,' she retorted, then slowly smiled again. 'I know next to nothing about you either, but it doesn't matter. We can still relax and enjoy our meal.'

For someone to be so straightforward was new to him. It went to show how jaded he'd become over the years. Amy often said he was in a rut and needed to get out amongst it—whatever *it* was. 'Sounds good to me.' He wasn't mentioning how different this was from his usual experiences with strangers.

'Aaron, where are you from?' someone asked.

'Edinburgh,' he answered.

'Have you worked outside Scotland before?' Bella asked.

'London for a year and Auckland for another when I was getting up to speed.'

'I lived in London for years,' she told him.

'Is that where you qualified as a paediatrician?'

'Mostly, yes.' Ask no more, her expression warned.

He wanted to delve deeper but there was

a stop sign blinking at him from her jade-coloured eyes. He got a lot of that with Bella, he realised. She was almost as reticent as him when it came to talking about herself. Which might mean something awful had happened to her at some point. Was that something to do with Jason? Again, he wasn't asking. Instead he stuck with the basics.

'We dragged her back here eighteen months ago,' Gino told him, obviously not concerned about Bella's need to change the subject.

'I can't imagine anyone dragging Bella anywhere she didn't want to go.'

'She did put up a fight,' Gino agreed. 'Tonight we're having lasagne. Hope that suits you?'

The subject was closed. Fair enough. 'Sounds wonderful, Gino.'

The man nodded once and headed back to his kitchen. Dinner confirmed, and Bella was relaxing.

Aaron's mind threw up a lot of questions. Why drag Bella back? She didn't appear to be a woman who depended on others to sort out her life. So something awful having happened that had the family rallying around to support her made sense. She'd said her husband died, and she might've struggled to the point she needed family to help her get back on her feet. It would be easier to watch out for her if she was here, not across the continent.

Bella's father leaned forward. 'So, Aaron, tell us about yourself. How many siblings have you got?'

Another change of subject. Talking about his family only wound him up but he'd give it a go as they'd been nothing but friendly and welcoming to him. 'One sister, Maggie. She's very busy and always telling me what to do. Not that I take any notice, but it's nice to get away at times.'

'What made you come to Stresa for the summer?' someone else asked. 'It's not usually a place where doctors come from other countries.'

'I can't see why not. It's beautiful, and not too big.'

Bella piped up. 'Aaron's only here for four months, then he's going back to Edinburgh.'

'He might not want to when his time's up. We live in one of the best places in Italy,' Bella's dad said.

Everyone laughed at that. 'Of course we do.'

He joined in the laughter and soon became immersed in fast banter that was hard to keep up with at times. Italians seemed to speed talk, or this family did anyway. At the same time they made him feel he'd been a part of them for a while.

'Let's take our coffee out on the deck,' Bella suggested when dinner was over and the children were being packed off to bed. 'Give you a break from this lot.'

'Good idea.' He picked up their cups and followed her out. Leaning against the railing, he peered down at the surrounding grounds. 'The gardens are amazing.'

'Papà spends a lot of time working in them. It's his passion now he's retired.'

'What did he used to do?'

'What do you think?'

'Chef?'

She nodded. 'He started out in a kitchen in a hotel in Roma with the dream of one day owning a small restaurant in the city. Then he met Mamma. She was a housemaid at the hotel and came from here. When they married she was already pregnant, so they moved to Stresa so

Nonna could help with the baby while they worked all hours getting a local restaurant up and running.'

'Gino was that baby?'

A small smile tugged at the corners of her lovely mouth. 'He started learning to cook when he was about eight. Apparently it was a battle to get him to go to school because there was nothing else he wanted to be but the best chef in Italy.'

Aaron sipped the strong coffee and sighed with pleasure. Perfect. 'So why did you choose medicine?'

'I don't know a lot about cooking.' She laughed.

Hearing that laughter lifted his spirits further. It was new to him and made her so much more approachable. 'Guess you didn't have to take your turn with prepping vegetables for dinner.' He'd never had to do so much as cook a piece of toast if he hadn't wanted to. There'd always been a housemaid and a cook in his family home. Sometimes he'd wondered if he might've been a different person if he'd had to make his own bed and stack the dishwasher every night. Not that he'd behaved like a spoilt brat. He hoped not anyway.

'There were still plenty of chores to do.' Bella sank back into her seat, holding her mug in both hands close to her breasts. 'You seemed to enjoy yourself over dinner despite my lot never shutting up.'

'It was fun.' Nothing like dinner at the Marshall house, even these days. He felt ridiculously comfortable with Bella's family. There was a sense of having found something he'd always hoped was out there but believed unavailable to him. He needed to stop thinking this way because in less than four months he'd be packing his bags and leaving, heading back to Scotland and the empty house he owned there.

'So you're feeling more relaxed now?'

He wasn't surprised she'd known how upset he'd been after that man had lost his rag over his wife's condition. He presumed that was her reason for inviting him to dinner. Not just a friendly invitation to a colleague. 'A lot better. Thank you.'

'Good.'

He liked how once again she didn't press for information, and seemed to accept he'd talk if he wanted and left him alone when he didn't. Which made it so easy to say, 'Five months ago

I was attacked in the emergency department where I worked in Edinburgh by a knife-wielding man on drugs. He believed he should be seen before anyone else although triage could find little wrong with him, apart from a broken toe.'

Bella shuddered. 'That's terrible. It's not uncommon for patients to think they should come first, but still.'

'Nor was the fact I was assaulted. But he stabbed me in the femoral artery. He seemed to know exactly where to strike. The fact I was in ED saved my life.'

Bella's hand covered his. 'No wonder you got uptight when that man lost his cool.'

'I feel bad now. There wasn't a weapon in sight.' There hadn't been last time either. Not initially. 'But it was an instant reaction to protect everyone in the vicinity.'

'I bet you'd have always done that.'

'True, I would have.' He stretched his legs out in front of him, enjoying Bella's hand on his. Such a simple touch, yet it filled him with wonder, and loosened some knots. 'The nightmares from that evening haven't gone away. They're why I don't sleep well.'

'Anything to do with why you came to Stresa to work?'

'Everything to do with it. I got burnout, and was always on edge at work. Still am, if I'm honest. The department head wanted me to take time off and go away for a long holiday. I prefer to keep busy, but not so much that I don't get to relax at work. I love what I do, but it became a chore. So I took on board what he said and looked for somewhere to work for a few months. I found the ad for the temporary position here and delved into it more. Once I learned the ED was in a small hospital and wasn't going to be anywhere near as busy as what I was used to, I applied.'

'And here you are.'

He turned his hand over, the urge to touch her overpowering his every protest, and wound his fingers around Bella's. 'Here I am.' She made him comfortable with her straightforward manner and allowing him to decide how much to tell her. No wonder it had been too easy to talk about what had happened and how he felt when he hadn't been able to do that with anyone else. Not once.

Bella turned to study him. 'We don't often

get aggressive people here. Today was a rarity. Tommaso told me in an aside when you were calming Signor Romano down that he's been known to lose his temper before. He doesn't always understand what's happening with his wife, whom he adores.' Her hand tightened around his. 'You were good with him. Firm but not nasty.'

The last of the tension gripping him from confronting the guy slipped away, replaced with relief and a new happiness. One he'd started to believe didn't exist for him. Lifting their joined hands to his lips, he kissed the back of Bella's. 'Thank you for listening and being so understanding.'

Pulling her hand away, with a hint of reluctance, she asked, 'Why wouldn't I?'

That was one question he definitely wasn't answering. He didn't want to spoil this tentative friendship by letting her know his background. If they got to spend more time together outside work over the coming months, then yes, he'd have to come clean because he didn't want to be thought of as a liar, but right now it felt so good to be accepted for who he was without all the hoo-ha attached. Bella Rosso was special. What was more, she made him feel special. 'Sometimes it's good to be accepted without having to explain yourself.'

She leaned closer, her face only inches from his. 'Now, *that* I understand.'

Why? He wasn't asking. That'd be doing what he appreciated her not doing. 'I'm glad.' It would be too easy to lean close enough to kiss her tantalising mouth.

Bella's eyes were large and focused entirely on him. What was she seeing? Thinking? Was she thinking? Could she read his mind?

'Bella?' Lifting his hands, he took her shoulders gently and pulled her a little closer, gazing at her exquisite features. 'You're beautiful,' he murmured, then jerked his head back. He was way out of line.

She stood up. 'I'd better help clear the table.'

'Sorry,' he said.

'Why?'

Damned if he knew.

Hey, wake up. She's carrying another man's baby. That's why.

He tensed. 'I think it's time for me to head back to my place.' He'd leave his car at the hospital overnight.

She nodded in agreement. 'I'll see you at work tomorrow.'

The near-perfect end to a wonderful night. Except it didn't feel close to perfect now that she'd cooled towards him a little. There was an ache going on in his chest. He wanted more time alone with Bella. Further talk so he got to learn more about her, to find out more about her husband, and that baby she was obviously carrying. Which was all plain frightening when he didn't do talking about himself, and he couldn't ask her to talk about herself if he didn't reciprocate. 'Goodnight.'

I want more time with Bella?

But she must be involved with someone else. Where was the guy anyway?

Aaron's steps were hard on the pavement as he grappled with the truth. He liked Bella Rosso a lot and she wasn't available.

CHAPTER FOUR

'ANDREA WANTS TO go home,' Gita told Bella the moment she stepped into the children's ward on Thursday. Andrea had only returned from Milan yesterday. 'Says his mother makes better pancakes than what he got this morning.'

'I bet she does.' Bella laughed. The hospital kitchen wasn't known for its gourmet meals. 'It's not up to me. When's Alec due to do his round?' The orthopaedic specialist came up from Milan two days a week and was due here today.

'He called to say he's on the early train so should be here any time soon, I'd say.'

'That'll make one small boy happy if nothing else.'

'Morning, Bella, Gita.' Aaron strode into the area looking relaxed and happy.

'Morning. What did you have for breakfast? I could do with some if it makes you so cheerful.' Her head was heavy and there was a nagging ache in her lower back. Hopefully not caused by the pregnancy this early on, or she'd be in for a lot more as the months continued. At fourteen weeks people were beginning to notice her baby bump and ask questions about how far on she was and how long she'd be working. Aaron hadn't asked anything, though she'd often caught him looking at her as if to make sure she really was pregnant. No doubt he'd be confused as to who the father might be. She'd tell him next time they were together, alone. Funny how she wanted him to know the truth behind her pregnancy sooner than later. She more than liked him and didn't want any shadows hanging over their friendship or whatever it might become.

If it became anything more. There was a lot to consider before that happened. The decision to have Jason's baby had been made knowing she'd struggle with any other man stepping into the father role. This baby was her last physical tie to Jason and, while she knew she was moving on from his death, a part of her couldn't let him go completely.

Aaron interrupted her thoughts. 'Toast and jam. Very boring, but it filled the gap.' He looked across to the room where four boys sat in their beds talking as if there were no tomorrow. 'I've just come from the canteen. Thought I'd pop in to see Andrea for a minute on my way back to ED.'

He'd visited the lad on her ward twice since he'd returned from Milan. Sometimes she wondered if it was an excuse to stop and say hello to her too. She was probably way off track. Just because his mere presence threw her nerves into a frenzy didn't mean he'd noticed her any more than he did any other women. But he always went out of his way to stop and talk to her.

'You're good doing that for him.' Even in this small hospital the ED staff didn't usually drop by to see a patient who'd been through their department. 'Andrea thinks the sun shines out of your backside.' Even she was starting to think there might be a ray or two. He was rather gorgeous, and kind, not pushy. Something that always sat well with her. *And* had her looking twice at him. No, that was because he was so attractive with that slight body and sexy face.

'I always like knowing how my patients are

getting on. I'm even more invested in Mattia and Andrea since we helped them at the accident scene.'

'I get where you're coming from. I always feel better knowing my patients' outcome.' It was part of being a doctor. Even when a patient walked out of the ward for the final time she still wondered how they were getting on. 'Working in Stresa means I often bump into my patients around town, which I like.'

'Not all of them are from around here though.'

'At the paediatric clinic I get referrals from Lake Como and a few from Milan.' That was something she was particularly proud of, people wanting to bring their children all the way up here to see her. Her share in the Paediatric practice within the hospital aligned to one in Milano was growing as word spread she was good at what she did.

'I did wonder how you could be so busy with only the hospital patients until Tommaso mentioned a lad staying in town with his grandparents who presented with early-stage leukaemia that you recognised and got him into the right specialist fast. His parents keep bringing him up here to you despite his cancer specialist being in Milan.'

'Yes, they do. I think it's their way of showing their gratitude for me finding out what was wrong with the boy when he presented with very few symptoms. I was only doing what I'm trained for and have had nothing to do with his treatment. The outcome is fantastic and makes me feel good about my small part in helping him.' Anton was back at school, playing football, hitting the grades in all his subjects and talking about becoming a doctor when he grew up.

'The reason we do what we do—getting the best outcomes for people suffering.' His smile was wide and genuine.

'When you two have finished patting each other on the back I have a prescription that needs finishing and signing, Bella.' Gita laughed. 'Her analgesics have run out,' she added.

I was doing that?

Bella swallowed as she felt her face heat. 'Right, move over and let me at the keyboard.'

The desk phone rang. Snatching it up, Bella said, 'Paediatrics, Bella Rosso speaking.'

'It's Tommaso. We've got a three-year-old girl presenting with vomiting and diarrhoea plus erratic heart rhythm. I'm thinking severe allergy reaction, cause unknown. She's on oxygen and her obs are not settling.'

'I'm on my way.'

'Bed three. Can you tell Aaron to get back too? It's gone crazy in here.'

'Done.' Slamming the phone down, she hurriedly filled in her code for the prescription Gita needed. 'I'm needed downstairs.' Then she was on her way, talking over her shoulder as she went. 'Aaron, you're required back in ED.'

A strong hand caught her wrist. 'Careful, you'll walk into the wall if you keep that up,' said Aaron. 'What's the hurry?'

His touch was warm and she shrugged him away. She wasn't even thinking about what that meant. She had a seriously ill child to worry about, not her reaction to a man's hand. But it was great. He felt hot, sexy. No, he didn't. Yes, he did.

'Bella?'

'A young child has presented with a severe allergic reaction.' A bee sting? Not likely or someone would've known. A child usually screamed blue murder when they were stung. A food the girl hadn't had before? Had she swallowed something that wasn't food? Or was it a reaction to a stray cat or dog causing the problem?

Bella all but flew down the stairs to ED with Aaron right beside her every step of the way. Which was kind of nice and made her feel special even when that was probably the last thing on his mind.

'Bella, this is Maria.' Tommaso stepped aside for her to get close to the bed where a small child lay curled up tight. 'This is her *papà*, Davido.'

The man looked terrified as he held his daughter's tiny hand in his large one. 'Do something, please.'

Bella noted the sweat glistening on Maria's forehead and cheeks, and the trembling all over her small frame. 'Has Maria ever before had any bad reaction to something she's eaten? Even a small one, like throwing up or even just wanting to? Feeling cold after eating something?'

'No. Nothing.'

'Blood pressure is low,' Tommaso told her. 'I've administered a light sedative to keep her calm.'

The tiny girl tried to roll into her father, and began crying when the oxygen tube hindered her.

'Where was Maria when this started?' Bella asked as she noted the raised body temperature on the monitor. 'What had she been doing before you found her?'

'She went with her big sister to the woods. About two hours ago. They came back when Maria was sick the first time.'

Woods. The ground would be soft and covered in leaves and grass. An image filled Bella's head. Mushrooms. Bright red ones. Poisonous.

'Davido, did you see the first time Maria vomited?' she asked urgently. When he nodded, she demanded, 'What colour was it?'

'Pink, reddish, I think.'

'I need a stomach pump in here fast. I know Maria's probably brought up most of her stomach contents but I need to be absolutely certain nothing's left.'

'Onto it.' Aaron was already moving, not

waiting for a nurse to do as Bella had demanded.

She'd been so focused on the little girl she hadn't even realised he was still with her. 'Are there mushrooms growing in those woods?' she asked the father.

His face turned ashen as he nodded. 'Sometimes. A few. But Maria wouldn't eat them. They'd taste awful.'

'Bright red, very pretty to a little girl.' Bella took the pump Aaron held out.

'Want a hand inserting it?' he asked.

'Can you remove the oxygen and hold her?'

Within minutes Bella was removing the pump. There'd been very little content in the stomach. 'That's a plus. Maria's already got rid of most of what caused the problem. Those few small dark pink pieces in the fluid look like they're from a mushroom. I'll send it to the lab for analysis, but in the meantime we need to draw some blood to check her liver and kidneys.'

'Is she going to be all right?' Davido asked as tears slid down his cheeks.

'Maria's fast reaction to the mushroom is good. I'm going with that being the problem, all right?' She didn't wait for an answer. 'Her heart is beating unevenly, and her blood pressure is low so we will move her to the ward where a nurse will be with her all the time. She'll continue to be on oxygen until everything settles down, as well as intravenous fluids since she's already lost a lot of fluid and at this age children get dehydrated very quickly.'

'You haven't really answered my question.' Davido was smart, as well as terrified for his daughter.

Bella's heart was filled with compassion. This had to be an absolute nightmare for any parent. 'I'll wait for the lab results for her liver and kidneys before I give you a definite answer, but I think Maria's going to be all right. Throwing up early on means the stomach didn't have time to absorb too much of the poison.'

'I need to talk to my wife. She'll be beside herself with worry. But she had to stay home with our other children.'

'Go outside where it's quieter and call her. I'll sit with Maria till you get back.'

Davido shook his head. 'I'm not going anywhere. I'm ringing from here.'

'I understand.' She wasn't leaving her patient

either. Pulling up a chair, she sank onto it and watched Maria breathing, slowly and unevenly, her tiny face all but obscured by the oxygen mask. 'The poor kid,' she said to herself.

'Who is very lucky her paediatrician was on the ball,' Aaron said quietly as he picked up the pump.

Glancing at him, she saw only respect in those beautiful winter-blue eyes. Warmth stole through her. Which it shouldn't. She didn't need his approval, but it felt so good getting it. 'It's frightening how easy it is for something so horrifying to happen.' Her hand touched her stomach. The downside to being a parent would be the constant worry about all the things that could go wrong. Being a doctor, she was more aware than most parents of what those could be.

'And how fast.'

'Sì,' she sighed. They were only saying what she'd said and heard often over the years of her career, but with Aaron it felt as though they were on the same page about more than just patient talk. More personal, as though they were each letting the other in a little bit. Did she truly want that? When she believed she'd

adjusted to living solo for ever? But then, letting Aaron in a little didn't equate to something deep and meaningful and long term. She leaned over Maria and studied her face. 'She's going to need lots of fluids.'

'We'll sort that before transferring her up to the ward.' He disappeared out of the cubicle, leaving Bella to catch her breath and put her out-of-sorts mind back in order.

Aaron managed to tilt her sideways ever so slightly without appearing to be aware of how he affected her. Which was a good thing, she reminded herself. The last thing she needed was a doctor she worked with thinking he was disturbing her like that. It could lead to all sorts of misunderstandings.

Though at the moment the only person not understanding the effect he had on her was herself. Why did her blood rush to her head whenever he came into the room? Why the sudden heat under her skin when he was beside her? Why the urge to reach out and hold him when he talked in that deep, sexy voice and his eyes sparkled with humour? A lot of questions she had no answers for, or answers she was prepared to take seriously. She had had her one love, and doubted she'd ever find another. Besides, in a few months he'd be gone and she wasn't moving away. London had been fun but it wasn't home.

Davido appeared on the other side of the bed. 'My wife says thank you for looking after Maria. She's so upset about the mushrooms and is going out right now to remove each and every last one she can find.'

'She'll have to check every morning until the season's over,' Bella said. 'Might be safer to talk to Maria and show her what made her sick in the first place. I can't imagine her ever wanting to eat a mushroom again, not even the good ones.' Which, considering how many people used mushrooms in their cooking, would cause a problem if she didn't learn to accept some fungi were safe.

Davido was gazing at his daughter, worry etching his face. 'We've been very lucky.'

Bella stood up. 'I'm just relieved we got to the cause quickly and there won't be any serious after-effects.'

A nurse appeared with a bottle of fluid and tubes to attach to Maria. 'Hey, little one, I'm going to give you a drink in the arm.'

Maria barely reacted to the nurse's words or the pressing sensation of the tube being attached to the needle already in place under her skin.

'She's exhausted,' Bella noted. 'I'll call the orderly to shift her to the ward where I can keep an eye on her.' Heading through the department, she couldn't help looking out for Aaron.

His deep voice coming from behind a curtain drawn around a bed was filled with concern. 'Signora Bianchi, you have fractured three ribs. You need to take medicine for the pain.'

The woman's reply suggested where Aaron could put the medication and it wasn't in her mouth.

Chuckling, Bella wondered how he'd deal with that response. She wasn't hanging around to find out. She was needed on the ward. But it was tempting to stay and listen to that voice that caused all sorts of unmentionable sensations to her body.

'Do you want to stay here all night?' Aaron asked calmly.

'No.'

Yes, thought Bella.

'Now, you see, here's the thing. The pain's going to cause you to lose sleep and be uncomfortable no matter what you're doing. A dose of pain-relief medication will help you move around and movement will help you feel better.'

Could the man sound convincing or what? Bella grinned as she hurried away. She'd do well to remember that in the coming weeks when they got together again over a meal at her family's home and restaurant.

So she was going to invite him more often? Why not? It was good having his company and he wasn't full of cheek and bossy like her brothers. Throw in how sexy and intriguing he was, and she realised she'd missed that. Was this disloyalty to Jason? Or more like getting on with her life?

'Feel like going for a walk along the lakeside after work?' Aaron asked Bella late Friday afternoon as she signed off a six-year-old who'd presented in the ED with a severe sore throat and swollen lymph glands.

Bella had ordered bloods done to confirm her suspicion of glandular fever. 'You're not looking for another dinner with my lot, by any chance?'

The thought had never crossed his mind. He didn't do looking for freebies. 'Not at all. I was thinking of asking you to join me for a beer and pizza in town,' he snapped.

Bella put her hand up in the stop sign. 'Sorry. I didn't mean to say you were a freeloader. It's because you seemed to enjoy yourself the other night that I thought you might like to do it again.'

His angst dropped away. So used to others expecting him to shout them meals or drinks, he hadn't stopped to think she might be making a kind gesture. 'It's me who should be sorry. I'm not used to being invited into other people's families.' Not for a meal with nothing expected in return, at any rate. He'd become such a cynic. It was a barrier formed from too many let-downs. Bella didn't deserve it. 'I'd love to share a meal with your family again some time but tonight I'd like to relax with you without having to be on my best behaviour.' To be able to enjoy her sexiness and stunning looks without worrying what her family might think.

Her eyes crinkled at the edges as she laughed,

sending his heart rate up a few notches. 'I'd love to go for a walk and work some kinks out of my back before we sit down to pizza and a drink. No beer for me, I'm afraid.'

Of course. The baby. 'Not a problem. I'm sure we can get some water.' He laughed. Doing more of that lately. Because of this woman? Or because he was working with a group of people who expected nothing more from him than his best medical abilities? Probably a mix of both, he decided.

'Give me ten minutes? I want to check up on a girl with bronchitis before I head out.'

'I'll change into some respectable clothes and wait for you in the car park. Don't hurry. We've got all night.'

When Bella blinked he realised how loaded that sounded. 'What I mean is—'

Her hand touched his shoulder. 'There's no rush. It's okay. I'm more than ready to get out of here. See you shortly.'

He missed her touch the moment she removed her hand. Plus the heady scent of roses she took with her as she strode to the elevator. She was doing his head in with that wicked laugh and those big eyes that didn't miss a thing. She was getting under his skin—that was what she was doing. Waking him up to possibilities he hadn't thought likely for so long. Hadn't wanted to consider at all. He liked keeping his heart safe. No, he didn't. It was hard work and brought no enjoyment, but it saved him from pain. Keeping it safe was the only way to go. Or he could leap off the edge and see how he landed. Maybe. Maybe not. A repeat of what Amy did was too awful to contemplate.

'Have a good weekend, Aaron,' Tommaso called as he went past. 'Forget you're an emergency doctor and have some fun.'

'I'll do my best.' Starting with a walk along the lakeshore with a delightful woman who seemed to like taking time out in quiet ways too. A bonus that came with working in Stresa was the stunning scenery. Throw in how small and friendly the town was and there was a lot going for this place.

'Any plans for the weekend?' Bella asked as they sauntered down towards Lake Maggiore.

'I thought I might drive up to the Alps. Go for a bit of a hike. Nothing too serious, just like to get out in the fresh air for a bit. What about you?' That idea had occurred as he gazed north. 'Would you like to join me? Though I suppose it's not a novelty for you.'

'I haven't been over that way for years. I used to do quite a bit of hiking in the mountains before I left to go to university in Milan. After that I never seemed to make the time to get away and I've missed it.'

That wasn't answering his question. 'Still got your boots?'

'I doubt it, but I do have sturdy walking shoes.' She tipped her head to look up at him. 'I'd love to join you if you don't intend being over-exertive.' Then the twinkle in those eyes vanished and she looked away. 'As long as we're not spending too much time together. I have to warn you I'm not interested in getting too close. I'm running solo these days.'

He should be pleased to hear that.

His heart was safe.

Not if the sudden thud in his chest was an indicator.

'Fair enough.'

She was still staring straight ahead as they continued walking. 'The thing is, I'm pregnant.'

'I'd surmised that.'

Her head shot up. 'How?'

'You do a little touch-the-tummy thing at times that I've seen with other pregnant women through the course of my work. You were also worried after that woman elbowed you out of the way at the accident.' Plus her tummy was slightly larger than what he'd expect for someone so slim.

'Yes, I was.' Bella blinked, then gave him a lopsided smile. 'No hiding anything from you, is there?'

'I wasn't aware you tried to.'

'I haven't. Not really. We're not so close I feel I should be telling you everything about my life.' Her breasts rose on an intake of air. 'But I might as well finish what I've started since you will probably join my family for a meal again some time and they're already asking if you know about the baby.' A blush coloured her face. 'Not that it's any of their business.'

Unable to resist that delicate look and bemused expression, Aaron reached for her hand.

Whoa. Getting too close, man.

Jerking his hand away, he kept walking along the pathway as though nothing felt wrong. 'They care about you.'

'They do. Too much sometimes but better than not at all.' Again she drew a breath. 'The thing is, I'm having Jason's baby. We knew his life expectancy was short once the myeloma returned after a year in remission so before he died he had his sperm frozen. We talked a lot about me being a solo mother, and the choice to go ahead with it was entirely mine.' She paused, then, 'I fell pregnant in his last year but sadly it wasn't to be.'

Aaron was gobsmacked. That had never crossed his mind when he'd wondered who the father might be. 'Hence Gino's protective streak.'

'Sì.'

'You're one very strong lady to be doing this.' She was also off-limits. Her late husband still meant so much to her she wouldn't be interested in getting close to another man.

'I don't always feel like it. Then I guess there'll always be days I'll feel incompetent even if I had a partner beside me.'

Did she want one? Seemed to him that her late husband had been her one and only. 'You waited a while. You did say Jason died three years ago?'

She nodded. 'I put my final year of qualifying on hold towards the end to nurse him so I wanted to finish that. I also kind of lost my way for a while. I think focusing so hard on study had me denying Jason had gone so I still had to grieve.'

When Bella opened up she certainly had no issues with telling him how she felt, and he felt special. Plus he was growing to care deeply for her.

'I reiterate—you are tough.'

'I hope so.'

'That's why your family's so important to you—for the days you're struggling.' If only his family had been the same. Instead they had never understood why he wasn't interested in being famous and wanting everyone to kowtow to him, and that he disliked being used for his wealth and who his family were. But he wasn't being fair. There was one person who'd understood him all along. 'You'd have liked my grandfather. He was my rock when I was a kid, always there if I needed someone to talk to. He let me be who I wanted to be.'

'What about your parents? You said mealtimes in your house were the opposite to my family, but surely there were times they'd sit down with you if you needed their help?'

See? Bella had a way of making him open his mouth and talk about things he always kept close to his chest. 'Not often.' That was all he was saying. Please. He could not tell this wonderful woman how he could be followed by the media whenever one of his parents or his sister made the news over their work.

'So your grandfather was your go-to person. At least you had him.'

'Yes. He always had time for my gripes.'

Bella glanced at him. 'Better than having no one at all.'

It was too easy to smile. 'Quite right.' His parents would've been there to listen if he'd decided to aim for the top of the best emergency specialists list, he thought. Though that did sound as if he were bitter, which wasn't true. He loved them and knew they loved him. It was only that he had different goals from theirs and his sister's. He'd excelled in his speciality but didn't make an issue of it. Sometimes he had to wonder if he really belonged to his family or had been adopted at birth. Of course he hadn't been. One look at his grandfather and anyone could tell he belonged to the Marshall clan, but still. 'I take it Jason was English?'

'London born and bred. I once suggested we move to Milan as I missed home. Of course, that wouldn't have happened as he didn't speak the lingo and therefore would've had problems with work, but there was no way he'd have left London anyway.'

'Why's that?'

'His career was going from strength to strength and he became well known and sought after. I understood he'd always aimed for that and couldn't expect him to give it away to move here.'

Sounded like anyone interested in Bella would have to accept living in Italy or not bother. 'You're home for good, then?' Another reason he'd stay on the sideline. He was returning to his home after this spell in paradise. Though when he thought about it, did he have to go back to Scotland? Why not settle somewhere else, in an area no one was so engrossed in his family's life that he couldn't get on with whatever he wanted uninterrupted? So far Stresa had been quiet in that respect.

Early days, warned his ever-wary mind.

'I am. I'm a partner in a great practice, and my child will have lots of family to support him or her.' Bella withdrew her hand and looked ahead. 'Where were you thinking of having pizza?'

Subject closed. Fair enough. He'd learned more than he'd expected and knew not to push the boundaries. He named a pizzeria he'd been to a couple of times. 'That suit you?'

'Perfect.'

He smiled, feeling more at ease than he had in a long time. Bella wasn't hard to please, and straightforward in her requirements. No expectations of grandeur…just took things as they came. He could get used to this. Which was another warning to walk away fast.

Only he didn't know how to do that.

Not true, Aaron.

He was very good at walking away. The problem was, he suddenly saw, he didn't want to. He hadn't felt this sense of bonding with a woman since he met Amy, and with Bella there seemed to be a depth to what was forming between them. Possibly because they weren't rushing into intimacy. As if that were likely to happen. She'd already pointed out she wasn't looking for a relationship. Strange how that made him stop and really look at her; how it had him wanting to know more and more about what lay behind that beautiful face and those intelligent eyes, and her determination to do this alone.

Bella Rosso was proving to be difficult to walk away from, even when they were only going for pizza.

Bella nearly tripped over her own feet, thinking about how Aaron accepted what she'd said without too many personal questions. After all the feedback—mostly unwanted—she'd had from others since announcing her pregnancy, he was a breath of fresh air. Not that he wouldn't have a head full of questions—he was human—but so far he was keeping them to himself.

'Grazie.'

'For taking you out for a pizza?' he asked with a cheeky grin on that handsome face. 'No problem.'

She let it go, relieved to have told him about the baby and Jason even when there was no serious reason she should. It was because they got on so well and seemed to be becoming friends that she wanted no secrets to get in the way. At least none that affected their day-to-day friendship. He didn't need to know how much she'd agonised over taking the final step to getting pregnant because once Jason was gone it didn't seem as straightforward as she'd anticipated. All the discussions they'd had about how she'd manage seemed superfluous now the pregnancy was real.

'Jitters,' Cara had told her on one of her indecisive days. 'You'll handle it brilliantly and on the days you don't we're all here for you.'

Yes, she was lucky with her family. Unlike Aaron, by the sound of it. How could his parents not want to be there for him? But then, she didn't know the story behind what he'd said, not even a fraction of it. 'Where did you learn to speak Italian?'

No one had a problem understanding him. He'd never have got the position at the local hospital if he hadn't been fluent in the language, but he didn't even have much of an accent. 'Growing up I had an Italian nanny until I was sent to boarding school. She came from Sorrento. She was very homesick for the first year and I was often alone and unhappy so she'd talk to me in her language and I'd copy her.'

Boarding school? A moneyed background to go with the good looks and great career? He didn't show off or flaunt it, if that was so.

'But you're fluent, orally as well as on paper. Or should I say on the screen?' She laughed. 'I'd have thought you'd need more than that to become as accomplished as you are.'

'Turned out I have an affinity for languages and Sara soon had me doing my homework in English for her to study and Italian for me to learn another language.'

'Where is she now?'

'Married to my old teacher and living in Glasgow. Seemed she got over her homesickness after coming to watch me in the school play.'

'A happy ending. I like it.'

'You're all for romances and everyone getting their happy ever after?'

'Of course. A little bit of romance never goes astray.' She'd had more than a little with Jason. They'd been the happy couple everyone wanted a piece of from the day they met over a bad pie in the hospital canteen in London when she'd been there for a month's training on a paediatric cancer ward. They'd never looked back. A wave of sadness rolled over her. Damn but she missed him. But she also knew she had to look forward now, possibly even find another man to share her and her child's life. If she didn't she'd still be all right, and would not spend every day thinking about what might've been if he hadn't died.

'I see.'

'Do you though?' She glanced up and saw Aaron's cheeky smile back in place. It turned her toes and made her heart beat wilder. Was it possible he could be her second chance? Except she didn't believe she'd ever love as deeply again. Nudging him with an elbow, she laughed. 'Don't tell me you haven't been in love and felt romance in the air.'

The smile slipped. 'Yes, I have. Obviously it didn't last for ever.'

Nor did hers, but it wasn't because Jason chose to leave. She touched Aaron. 'I'm sorry to hear that. Life can be a bitch at times.'

'It sure can, but looks to me like you've found it can also be wonderful. When's baby due?'

Subject moved from him back to her. Fair enough, though it was unlike her to talk about herself so much. Another clue that she might be getting more involved with Aaron than was wise. He was only here for a few months while she was home permanently. Moving back to Britain wasn't an option. Italy was home for her. 'Early November.' Her hand touched her stomach.

How's it going in there?

'It's quite exciting really.'

When she wasn't worrying about how she'd manage baby and her career despite her family saying they'd be there for them.

'After I've left Stresa, then.'

'Sì.' Something she should remind herself of whenever she started to think how wonderful he was. 'Unless we wow you over so that you become a permanent member of the hospital staff.'

He shook his head. 'I'm still under contract in Edinburgh. This is a break, nothing more.'

'Point taken.'

This man knows what he's doing.

She should follow his example. Nothing changed because he was so sexy and exciting.

'I am enjoying working in a close-knit community. There's something special about the people around here. You all seem to stick up for each other no matter the cost to yourselves.'

Exactly why she loved home. 'Wouldn't you?' She'd read him entirely wrong if his answer was no.

'Absolutely, but not everyone I know is the same.' His mouth had tightened, warding off her next question. Was he talking about his own family? From his few comments about them it was more than likely.

Tempting as it was, she didn't ask. He might cancel dinner and she'd be gutted. His company was enjoyable, and something she hadn't had in a long time apart from her family, which wasn't the same. Not that she'd been looking very hard. The few dates she'd tried might've been about testing the waters but she hadn't been overly enthused. Yet somehow Aaron managed to wake her up to start looking around at her world.

Looking at him, more like, she told herself with a soft chuckle. 'Not everyone's perfect around here either.' But the ones closest to her were and she knew how lucky she was. Hopefully she gave back as much as she received.

Suddenly the tiredness she'd been fighting all day filled her and made her legs feel lifeless. 'Are we walking to the pizza place or going back to get our cars first?' The pizzeria was closest.

'Let's go eat first. We can always grab a cab afterwards if necessary.'

With a bit of luck, dinner would re-energise her so she was up to the return walk, at least as far as home. The car would be safe at the hospital overnight if need be. 'Works for me.'

'Glad to hear that. My stomach's starting to get impatient for food.'

Hopefully hers would feel the same soon. She did need to keep up her intake for baby. There were days when she struggled eating three meals. The midwife said she'd get past that soon. Right now energy was a requirement so she had to eat. Force-feed herself if necessary. 'Nothing worse than a hungry man.'

CHAPTER FIVE

'SORRY, BUT I'M not going walking with you today. I've had a sleepless night and don't feel one hundred per cent this morning,' Bella told Aaron over the phone the next morning.

'You were shattered last night. Why didn't you sleep well?' Was this normal for Bella or was there something wrong? It was the beginning of the weekend and she didn't have to go to work.

'I've had a few nights like that since I became pregnant.' She hesitated, as though tossing up whether to say any more. 'To be expected, I suppose.'

He wasn't buying it. 'Have you talked to someone about this?'

'Aaron, I'm fine.'

'And I'm a concerned colleague. And friend,' he added because colleague didn't explain his feelings about her. 'How's your blood pressure?'

'Normal.'

'When did you last check it?'

'Aaron, stop it. Go enjoy your walk in the hills. I've got chores to do.' *Click.* Gone.

'Well, Bella Rosso, I've got more important things to do than go walking. I'm coming to visit you and make sure nothing serious is wrong.' He tossed his phone on the table and picked up the bowl of breakfast cereal he'd been eating when she called. The problem being he wasn't Bella's doctor and had no grounds for checking her out. She could very easily kick him off the property without talking to him. Gino would be right behind her if he upset the chef's sister.

But he wasn't about to ignore the need to make sure Bella was all right. He had to know, to help her if necessary. Just as her family would if they knew.

He'd had a cab drop Bella back at her apartment after they'd finished pizza last night. She'd looked tired beyond belief and hadn't argued when he'd told her he was calling up a ride for her. Something that should've told him she wouldn't be walking today, but he'd been too happy in her company to think about this morning. A simple meal in a noisy pizzeria filled with locals celebrating the end of the working week, and he'd relaxed so much he'd felt a different man, almost as though he'd found a town he felt totally at home in.

But he had noticed Bella's exhaustion. Hard not to when dark shadows stained her cheeks beneath those usually gleaming eyes. It hadn't been only the doctor in him keeping an eye on her. He wanted to make sure nothing was wrong. He cared about her. Probably looking for signs of a deepening friendship that weren't there. Deepening friendship or something more? No, couldn't be anything more. Mustn't be.

He was returning to Edinburgh at the end of this contract.

You don't have to.

Yes, he did. He owed it to his colleagues after all they'd done to help him through the aftermath of nearly losing his life. He also had his dream career there.

Plus he was still having the nightmares and until they were gone he had to concentrate on sorting himself out. It wouldn't be fair to dump his problems on Bella. Nor did he want her knowing how screwed up he'd become since that attack, though after his reaction to Signor Romano she probably had some idea of that.

But the biggest issue standing between them getting close was that she was having her late husband's baby. She was comfortable with what she was doing and didn't need another man in her life sharing her child. Or did she? Behind her brave face she might be in a right old state about raising a child on her own, yet it wouldn't be easy to let another man who wasn't baby's dad into her life.

Yet the most important reason for not getting close and falling for Bella was that she did not need all the publicity that went with being a member of his family. He wasn't implying she'd become his wife. Not yet anyway. If ever. But she didn't have to for the media to start chasing her down and asking questions that were none of their business. If they did fall for each other, what was to say she wouldn't wake up one morning and walk away when it all got too much? Because it would. It always did. Amy had done it when she'd been his support system, and said how much she believed in him—and loved him.

So he had to stay away from Bella. After he made sure she was all right.

Snatching up the keys to his car, he headed over to see Bella.

Gino opened the side door to the stairs Aaron presumed led to the upstairs apartments. 'Hey, Aaron, you here for Bella?'

'Thought I'd drop by.' Lame, but Bella would be furious if he mentioned her being so tired. Gino might already know but he suspected not. She tried to keep worrisome things from her family.

'You've just missed her. She's gone to pick up her car and then to see a friend out Orta way.'

Great. Had she figured he'd come round? 'No worries. I'll catch up with her some time over the weekend.'

'You could call in after lunch,' Gino said. 'She'll be back by then.'

Because I'm meant to be walking the hills all day.

As she well knew. He should go do it. The idea had been very appealing yesterday, even this morning until he'd learned he'd be doing it alone, and now it was the last thing he wanted to do. 'I might just do that,' he told Gino before heading back to his car. In the meantime he'd stock up on groceries and other bits and pieces he required.

'Aaron,' Gino called. 'Bella looked a bit pale this morning. Can you check her out without letting her know what you're doing?'

His heart swelled at the thought this protective brother trusted him to look out for his sister. 'Already onto it.'

Gino stared at him, but only nodded before he finally turned away.

This family was drawing him in, like it or not. Truth was he did like it. Just didn't know how to go with this because someone would end up getting hurt. The last person he wanted that to happen to was Bella. She did not deserve it. Nor did he but he knew the risks. She didn't. Except now he could not walk away from Gino's challenge. Because the man was setting him up to see how he fared. 'See you later,' he called as he opened his car door. He got no reply, which wasn't a surprise.

* * *

'What happened to your walk?' Bella asked when she opened her door to him mid-afternoon.

'Changed my mind about going and did a few other less exciting but necessary chores around town.' Those dark shadows were still darkening her face. 'Coffee?' He held up a cardboard tray with two paper mugs.

Suspicion blinked out at him from tired eyes. 'What's this about?'

He wasn't going to get past the door until he told her, and he wasn't going to lie. 'You're exhausted, too much even for a busy week in your current condition. I want to make sure there's nothing untoward going on, Bella.'

She gave him the same stare Gino had earlier in the day. She didn't like anyone interfering with her life.

He was going to be sent on his way.

Then she slowly stepped back. 'Come in.'

Surprised, and relieved, he followed her into a bright, sunny apartment with cream furniture piled with cushions in every colour of the rainbow. 'I like it.' The warmth and homeliness made him smile.

'I'm not a monochrome kind of girl.' She slowly returned his smile. 'That coffee smells good. Just what I need to perk me up.'

It was an opening to press her for more info on how she was feeling, but Aaron also saw caution in her countenance. 'Me too.'

She sat on the couch while he took a chair further away. Popping the top on his coffee, he sipped tentatively. 'What have you been doing this morning?'

'I went to see a friend I've known since school days. Didn't stay long as her kids were needing various things done and she really didn't seem to have time to sit for even five minutes.'

'Does that worry you for the future? Having to cope with a busy child on your own?'

Her laugh was brittle. 'I'll leave worrying about that while I get through the baby phase first.'

Aaron winced. She wasn't in a good place right now. Placing his coffee on the side table, he turned to face her, and took her hand into his. 'Talk to me, Bella. You're tired, and sounding flat.' Lonely was another word that came to mind but he kept it back. 'I've got broad shoulders.'

'I've noticed,' she quipped, but her face didn't lighten.

'Then use them.' *Any way you like.* Silence fell.

Bella appeared to be contemplating how far to trust him. 'It was a big decision to make about having our baby,' she said.

He relaxed. 'Any regrets?'

Her hair flicked back and forth on her shoulders. 'None at all. It was hard getting the positive result and not having Jason there to celebrate though.'

'I can imagine.' It was going to be even harder giving birth without him at her side. 'One step at a time.' Becoming a parent wasn't something he dwelled on. Opening up to finding the right woman to share that experience with came first. Bella? Right now he needed to focus on her and her physical concerns. 'Have you been more tired than usual lately?'

'Only over these past couple of days. My back's aching and I get the odd sharp pain in my stomach.'

'Have you talked to your midwife?'

'She says to rest and let her know if nothing improves.' The eyes Bella turned on him were filled with concern. 'She knows what she's doing but that doesn't stop me worrying myself sick.'

'Any blood spotting?'

'No.'

'Show me where the pains occur.'

Her hand tapped her lower stomach on the left side. 'Which doesn't make a lot of sense.'

No, it didn't, but sometimes pain didn't always hit where it came from. 'Can I check your BP?'

She nodded. 'My medical bag's in the bottom of my wardrobe.'

'I'll get it?'

'Do you mind?'

'Not a bit.' She was accepting his help. That was what mattered. He got the bag and removed the monitor.

She held her arm out. 'So far I've never had high blood pressure, but pregnancy can interfere with that.'

'You're a worried mother-to-be and a doctor to boot. They say doctors and nurses make the worst patients.' A minute later a relieved sigh slid across his lips. 'Normal. Which, given how worried you are, is a bit of a surprise. Have you had back problems prior to getting pregnant?'

Another nod. 'I once had a severe sprain in the lower region after a skiing accident that sent me tumbling down the slope while entangled with another skier. That was about eight years ago.'

'Spinal injuries are notorious for recurring. Though I'd have expected it to cause trouble further along with your pregnancy when you're carrying weight at the front, not now so much.'

'The pain's to the front, remember? And it's not constant. Just the occasional stab.'

'I think you're having minor tweaks that come with your body adjusting to the pregnancy, but, for peace of mind, let's get you thoroughly checked over, internally and externally. Ask your midwife to meet us at the hospital. Or we can see one of the doctors in the emergency department. Your call.'

He was all right with the external work, but would not do anything else. They were friends. Some things were best left for the professionals, which in this case he didn't feel he was. So much for keeping space between them. He was being wound in closer and closer like a salmon on the line, and resisting was impossible. Especially when Bella needed him.

'Thank you for understanding. I'm being a worry-wart at the moment, but I miscarried four years ago so a check-up might shut up my nagging fears, though you've already shut down most of them,' she said with a little smile. A more relaxed smile than he'd seen so far today.

'Come on. I'm driving.'

'I wouldn't have expected anything else.' Now her mouth curved upward and some of the tension in her face disappeared. Then she blushed. 'Now you won't think I'm the strong woman you first thought.'

Taking her shoulders in his hands, Aaron gazed down at this woman who already had him wondering if he might change his life for something better. 'Bella Rosso, wash your mouth out. Don't ever think like that. Even the strongest have moments when they're uncertain. You want this baby. You're ready to give up so much for it. I'm sure your feelings are perfectly normal. If they aren't then you're setting a new trend.' He held back from brushing a light kiss on her forehead and growled, 'You've got this.'

Now let's get the hell out of here and get you checked over before I make a complete fool of myself by hauling you into my arms and kissing you until neither of us can stand through the need filling our bodies.

Make that until *he* couldn't, because he didn't have a clue how Bella might feel. She'd probably slap his face if he tried to kiss her.

She was still gazing at him, but now the tip of her tongue was moving across her bottom lip. 'Aaron?'

'Yes,' he managed around the sudden desire in his throat.

'You're special.' Then those full lips were on his mouth and her tongue was tasting him.

He was special? Because he supported her? Believed in her? Heat swamped him, had him deepening his kiss. 'You're the special one,' he whispered as his arms wound around that stunning body and brought her close to him, so close her breasts pressed into his chest and her thighs were hard against his legs, and that small baby bump was pushing into his gut.

Baby.

Bella's and her late husband's. Not his. Nothing to do with him. Flipping his head up, he lowered his arms and stepped back. 'Bella—'

'Yes, sorry, I guess this is all wrong. You're being kind and I got carried away.' She walked out of the apartment, leaving him behind.

'Bella, wait.' He went after her.

'It's all right, Aaron. I understand,' she threw over her shoulder.

'No, you don't. Hell, I don't.'

That made her stop and turn around, a bemused look on her face. 'Not used to being kissed out of the blue?'

'More like not used to not knowing what to do.' Bella was getting to him in unprecedented ways.

'Now what?'

He drew a long breath. He'd love to haul her back into his arms and continue that mind-blowing kiss, followed by another and another. 'We'll get you checked over and then we'll see where we go from there.' He hesitated.

Go on, say it. Tell her you want her.

No, they weren't ready. He wasn't anywhere near ready. Might never be.

* * *

'We'll see where we go from there,' Aaron had said. Back to her apartment for another kiss? Despite the exhaustion dragging at her, that was where she'd like to go, but Bella knew it wasn't happening. She should be grateful Aaron had come to his senses and pulled on the brakes, but she wasn't. Not a bit. It was the first kiss she'd had in years that she hadn't wanted to walk away from. The men she'd dated hadn't stirred her blood or made her excited.

Aaron did that without even trying. Now she'd kissed him she wanted more. But it wasn't happening. She was going to have a baby and start a different life that probably wouldn't enthral him at all.

'Let's get this over with.' It might be best to go alone but she needed his support. He was a doctor so would keep her grounded if there was a problem. He wouldn't wrap her up in cotton wool and tell her what she couldn't do. For a few blissful moments with him she'd forgotten her concerns about the baby and her exhaustion, which showed how much he disturbed her equilibrium. 'Let's go.'

'Do you lock your apartment?'

Her shoulders sagged. How had she forgotten that? She didn't leave the door wide open for just anyone to wander in. The kids had no barriers at times. 'Not always but I've left my handbag behind.'

'I'll wait here.'

Staying safe from her? Fair enough. If she could kiss him without warning, then who knew what else she was capable of? Except she'd just had a quick, short lesson on how to behave around Aaron. They might be getting involved, but he wasn't keen on knowing her too well.

Snatching up her bag and phone, she closed the door and headed for the lift, Aaron beside her. Protective to the core, that was him. Plus genuine, caring and the sexiest man she'd been lucky enough to meet since she'd found herself single again. Lucky or unlucky? Because now it was going to be hard to remain casual around him at all times. Even when she wasn't actively looking for a man to have fun with. She was carrying Jason's child, which was a huge barrier to letting someone into her life.

Aaron opened the door for her when they reached his car. How many men did that these days? Sinking into the seat, she buckled herself in, and drew a breath as he got behind the steering wheel. 'Why did you really change your mind about going hiking? You were quite excited yesterday.'

The engine roared to life.

'It didn't appeal as much after you cancelled.' Blunt but honest.

'I couldn't have walked to the end of our drive this morning,' she told him. 'I barely made it round the supermarket, and when I got to my friend's house I was almost glad she didn't have the time to sit down over a coffee with me.' As long as the tiredness was normal for this stage of her pregnancy then she'd relax, but not until she was certain.

'I'm not having a poke at you, Bella. I'd have been more upset if you'd joined me because you felt you had to. I'll do the walk another day, with or without you.'

So they were still friends. Which sounded childish, but these days she couldn't always be certain she understood men. One she'd dated had got uptight because she didn't want an affair with him, and accused her of using him because he was rich. He'd shocked her because he'd seemed a quiet man who only wanted to share a meal or go to a show with a friend. Another told her she was too boring after saying how excited he was at going to the theatre with her.

'I'd like that. I promise to eat lots of energy bars the night before.'

'Don't you dare. We'll go if and when you're up to it, not because you've had a sugar overload.'

'Yes, boss.'

'Better believe it.' He was laughing.

Which took the edge off her fear that she might've lost a friend when she kissed him. Aaron had only come into her life very recently but already she couldn't imagine not having him there in some capacity.

'Who's on duty this weekend?' The emergency department sometimes struggled to provide enough doctors over the busy summer period now in full swing.

'Tess took today and Tommaso is on tomorrow.' He glanced her way briefly. 'You okay with Tess?'

'As in a female doctor to check me out? Absolutely. We get along fine workwise. Someone has to deflect the male medics' cheeky comments at times and I support her whenever I hear them.' It was all in good fun as the staff got on well, but she was glad Tess would be there. Everyone had warned her she'd lose all her inhibitions now she was pregnant, but to do so with a male colleague seemed harder to handle. She knew she was being precious but she was allowed some pride.

'When did you last have your haemoglobin tested?' was Tess's first question.

'I can't remember.' Bella thought back as far as possible and shook her head. 'There's been no reason to.' She never got sick.

'Then guess what? Today's as good a day as any to take a blood sample. Plus we need to know your iron levels. They're the first to take a hit when you're pregnant.'

'I'm not quite four months on.' Iron deficiency tended to happen more in the third trimester. Anyway, her diet was healthy, no reason for low iron levels. Her doctor brain kicked in. Diet wasn't the only cause. Internal bleeding was another. 'Take the sample.'

'Have you had an ultrasound yet?'

'No. I keep meaning to make the appointment but it never seems to work out with my work schedule.'

'It's your lucky day. The radiology technician on duty is qualified to do them so we'll get one done this afternoon.' Tess was smiling as she felt around Bella's abdomen. 'This feels fine, but better to be safe. Right, knees up, I'll do an internal before phoning Radiology.'

'All good so far,' Bella told Aaron when she was dressed again. 'Tess has arranged for me to have an ultrasound so if you need to get away I'll phone one of the sisters-in-law to pick me up afterwards.'

'I'm not going anywhere until you're ready to go home.'

She hadn't realised how tense she was until he said that. 'Thanks.'

'Want company while they slide the camera through the goo on your stomach?'

Her eyes widened as she looked at him. 'You'll come with me?'

'If it makes you happy to have someone with you, then yes.'

From all accounts it wasn't an uncomfortable

procedure but what if something was wrong? 'I'd like that,' she said quietly, suddenly frightened of what might be happening. It didn't feel strange accepting his offer. His support would help a lot.

Aaron took her elbow. 'Let's do this so you can relax and feel better.'

He seemed to have no hesitation about being seen with her in the hospital. It wasn't bothering her either. They were adults, free to do as they pleased. Not friends with benefits but friends in a good, caring way. She managed a small laugh. It had been so long since she'd felt the touch of a man. Until Aaron she hadn't wanted to, and now she didn't want him to pull away. That kiss had hyped her up. Something exciting was happening. 'More likely I'll fall asleep when the pressure's off.'

'Talk about exciting.' Aaron grinned, unaware he'd repeated the same word that explained her sudden happiness. Exciting did it every time.

'I know. Watching paint dry would be more fun.' She turned into Radiology, then hesitated. 'What if…?'

'We'll sort it, whatever it is.'

She shivered. The excitement was gone. There were some conditions that couldn't be sorted. Yet when she looked to Aaron she saw his strength and belief in her and instantly calmed. He'd told her she was strong, and it was true. She'd come this far following Jason's death and now wasn't the time to stumble. 'You're right. I will.'

'Think I said *we* will.'

She had no answer. She liked he'd said that even though it was too soon to be including him in everything tied to her pregnancy. Or her life. She was running solo. Which didn't explain why she felt good having him at her side right now.

Together they watched the screen as the technician scanned her uterus. Bella's heart rate had increased from the first moment the wand touched her stomach, and she reached for Aaron's hand.

'Nothing out of order,' said the young woman. 'But a radiologist will read the results on Monday to be absolutely certain.'

'I'm not miscarrying?'

'No. Baby looks very comfortable in there.'

She couldn't ask for more than that. This

woman would've done hundreds of ultrasounds and know what she was looking at. 'I feel better already.' Surprisingly, she did.

'Do you want to know the sex of your baby?'

Bella hesitated. In the beginning she'd thought she'd wait until the baby was born, but lately she'd started thinking she'd like to have a name ready the moment she laid eyes on him or her. 'Yes, I think I do.'

'Want me to leave you alone?' Aaron asked.

'Not at all. If you're happy to stay, then I'm happy to have you here.'

Wow, they were getting in deep.

It's the baby's sex, not a binding agreement to spend the rest of our lives together.

'Thank you.'

She was doing him a favour? Or was he feeling close to her and wanting to be involved in everything? Too soon, yet she couldn't tell him to go. Her hand tightened around his. She wanted him here more than just about anything. She'd think about that later. 'Right, let's find out.'

More goo and pressing from the wand and soon Bella was staring at the image on the screen, a tear trekking down her cheek. 'A girl?' Not a boy from what she could see in the grey picture.

'A girl.' The tech nodded as she pressed print. 'Here's the first photo of your daughter.'

Bella stared at the image, barely able to take it all in. 'That's my baby,' she whispered.

Aaron rubbed her back in slow, soft circles. 'Yes, Bella, that's your daughter.'

The technician stood up. 'I'll leave you for a moment to take it all in.'

More tears escaped. 'I'm having a daughter. Sophia Justine.' The names spilled out with no input from her brain, though Sophia was her grandmother's name and Justine was Jason's mother's.

'You'd already thought of names?' Aaron asked.

'No, those just happened.' Sort of. They had been playing around in her mind on and off. She paused, breathed deep. 'But I like them. Really like them.'

'Sophia Justine, eh? Well, little girl, you grow big and strong for your *mamma*.' Aaron looked away, but not before Bella saw a tear appear at the corner of his eye.

'You ever thought of having kids?'

'Who doesn't?' He was talking to the wall. Not a defining answer, but he'd said yes in his own way.

'It's natural to want to be a parent. That's the easy bit. Finding the right other half to do it with is harder, and then there are all the other considerations. To work or not, to want one or more, where to send them to school. The list goes on and on.'

Be quiet, Bella. You're overdoing it.

Now Aaron looked at her. 'I didn't realise you spent so much time thinking about it. But then I shouldn't be surprised. You like to be prepared, if nothing else.'

'I also like some surprises every now and then,' she said a little too acerbically.

'I wasn't criticising. I'm in awe of how you manage your work, and plan for your child's future so that it will go well.'

'Isn't it what all expectant parents do? You can't have a baby without some forethought.'

'True. I'd be much the same if the opportunity arose.'

The sadness in his voice had her wanting to reach for his hands but she sensed he wouldn't thank her. He seemed to be in a bubble of his own. 'You never know what's around the next corner, Aaron.' That applied to good and bad events, but she wasn't saying so. 'If you're open to accepting whatever comes along, that is.'

'So if a woman with six kids and a horse is around the corner waiting for me I'm to leap in and invite them to my home, never to let them out of sight again?' he asked, smiling.

'Absolutely. Your place would probably be more spacious than their caravan.'

'You always know how to cheer me up, don't you?'

She wasn't aware of that. 'Glad to be of some help.' A yawn ripped out of her. 'Can you give me a lift home? I feel even more shattered now I know nothing's seriously wrong.' It was as though she'd let go the last worry holding her together and wanted nothing more than to curl up and sleep.

'Your place or mine? I've got a comfortable sofa and I can whip up a light meal while you take it easy, if you'd like.'

She didn't have to think about it. 'If I go home I'll have to tell the family they're getting a granddaughter and a niece and then there'll be no end of talk and everyone dropping in to let me know how they feel, which will only be good, but I'm not ready for them just yet.'

'My place, then.' He tugged her to her feet, put an arm around her waist. 'Let's go.'

It was too easy to snuggle in close to that firm, warm body and let Aaron take charge for a little while. Too easy and right now she didn't care.

Aaron wrapped a light blanket around Bella as she slept on the sofa. She'd barely touched the tuna salad he'd made, and even her cup of tea had gone cold without a sip being taken.

'You're beautiful,' he whispered. A strand of dark hair lay on her cheek, tempting him to lift it away, but he refrained. If she woke because of his action he'd be in deep trouble, even if they'd edged closer over the afternoon. If only he could hold her in his arms while she snoozed the evening away.

She'd let him stay for the scan. Seeing that baby image was beyond description. His heart had swelled and he'd felt a tug of love for Bella's child. It had been an incredible moment that he wasn't likely to ever forget.

He couldn't remember when a woman had

sneaked under his radar so effortlessly. Apart from Amy and he wasn't going there. He'd always been alert to being used by anyone he encountered, and especially the women who appeared nonchalant around him only to be trying to win him over. Amy hadn't done that. Nor did Bella. She treated him as she did everyone—by accepting him for who he was and not trying to change anything.

Except she doesn't know who you are.

Therein lay the problem. One day—and that was getting nearer every hour they spent together—he was going to have to fess up, and hope like mad she still accepted him for who he truly was. Not only an emergency specialist and a keen hiker who enjoyed a bowl of good pasta and sitting on his deck having a wine, and who, yes, one day did want a family of his own, but the rest as well. Son of wealthy parents famous for their careers and social life, and brother of an aspiring camerawoman fast making a name for herself who also loved being in the spotlight and sharing everything about her life with anyone who'd listen. He really was the odd one out in his family.

Aaron walked out onto the deck and leaned

against the railing to stare at Lake Maggiore as the sun went down. Stunning came to mind. He could go a long way before finding anything else quite so breathtaking. He was probably biased because of the woman lying on his sofa. She added to the mystic beauty of this area. He'd never again think of Stresa without thinking about Bella. In his mind they went hand in hand. He was smitten with them both.

His gaze dropped to the semi-ruin covered with ivy on the opposite side of the road. There'd be history behind those walls. Like the local hospital with its stone walls evoking a sense of awe in him. It underlined how comfortable he'd become so quickly in Stresa. The people were friendly and never in such a hurry they didn't stop to say hello, making him think he belonged in a way he'd never known.

He was nowhere near ready to return home, even if he could get out of the four-month contract, which he wasn't prepared to try because that'd mean letting the hospital down, as well as all the staff who'd welcomed him with open arms and whom he got on with very well.

Nor had the nightmares abated. He hadn't been here long, but he'd hoped there'd be some sign they would go by now. A good reason not to go to sleep while Bella was here. The last thing he needed was her hearing him crying out in the middle of the night. She might know about the stabbing, but she had no idea just how badly it had screwed with him.

Mind you, with Bella within range the chances of him sleeping were zero anyway.

The air shifted around him and Bella was there, standing beside him, looking in the same direction as he was. 'Magic, isn't it?'

'Yes.' The lochs at home were equally stunning, but it was the warmth and relaxed atmosphere here that got to him. Bella added to his enjoyment.

'I should be getting home.' Not a lot of enthusiasm going on in her voice.

'Sure you want to?' he asked.

She turned to lean back against the railing and locked those sensual eyes on him. 'Not really.'

Drawing a quiet, slow breath, he lifted the strand of hair away from her cheek to tuck it behind her ear. 'We have some unfinished business that I'd like to see through to the end,' he said quietly, watching her closely.

‘We do.’

They continued to look at each other, the silence and expectancy drawing out between them. They reached for each other in the same instant, hands gripping each other, mouths meeting, opening; tongues touching and entwining. She tasted wonderful. She felt sublime in his arms, against his tight body. She smelt of roses and sun and life. A different life. A promise that hadn’t been made but might come true if he opened up to it.

He knew he was risking everything he’d spent a lifetime trying to save, but for once he had no control over his emotions. Or he didn’t want to control them. They’d started running rampant when he’d seen that image of her baby daughter and the tears pouring down her face as love warred with fear of getting it all wrong in her eyes. ‘Bella?’

‘Sì?’

‘Stay the night with me.’

‘Sì.’

There was nothing more to say. Any other words would spoil the magic surrounding them, isolating them from everything and everyone else. Lifting her into his arms, he strode inside and along to his bedroom, where he placed her gently on the bed.

'I'm not made of glass.' She laughed and bounced up to hold his head while she planted a long, intoxicating kiss on his mouth.

When he finally came up for air, he was rock hard and pulsing with need for her. 'Steady. We don't have to rush.'

'Can't see me being able to go any slower. I want you, Aaron. Now.'

'Not happening.' As much as he was struggling to keep control of his own desire, he was not diving in without first pleasuring Bella. 'First time I've known you to be impatient.' He grinned as he began unbuttoning her blouse and exposing the sexiest breasts he'd ever seen. His hard-on got harder and his pulse felt as if it were about to explode.

Added to by the hot sensation of Bella's hands on his waist, unzipping his shorts and pushing them lower. Sliding inside his pants and finding his need, wrapping around him, squeezing, caressing, turning his head to a molten mess. But not quite enough to hand over to her. 'Bella, wait.' When she didn't stop, he begged, 'Please.'

'Touch me.'

His hands lifted those hot breasts, his fingers tweaking the hard nipples.

'Lower.'

He deliberately took his time feeling her breasts and leaning in to kiss each one thoroughly before kissing a light trail between them and down to her belly. His tongue tasted her left and right, up and lower. His hands felt the tension tightening in her body as she cried out to be taken.

Sliding further down the bed, he found her sex, licked it until she was pushing upward and crying out louder. When he slid his finger inside, her whole body shuddered.

Bella shoved her fingers through his hair, caught his head and pulled him away. 'No, no more licking or I'll come. I want you in me for that.'

He was more than ready. So was Bella. Her hot, wet sex took him in, tightened around him as she rocked her hips upward. And he dived deeper into the heat, only to pull back and press in again and again, until he was out of his mind with need and Bella was crying out and shuddering all around him. Then he let go, and joined her in wonder.

Later they lay spooned together, with Aaron's arm over Bella's waist, his hand splayed over her baby bump. It felt wonderful. The most natural thing in the world, and it wasn't his baby. His hand tensed.

Bella covered it with hers. 'Relax. It's all right. We haven't done anything wrong.'

No, but the baby was beginning to intrude on his happiness. Not because he didn't want it there, but it indicated lots of issues lying between them. Important problems he wasn't prepared to ignore. Nor was he ready to take them on and tell the world to go to hell because Bella would get hurt if he did, and she was the last person he wanted to upset. She was too important to treat as a one-night stand. Or to have a brief fling with. Too late. They'd already started something. He rolled onto his back and put his hands behind his head, stared up at the semi-dark ceiling. 'You're right, we haven't. But I hope we haven't spoilt a great friendship.'

'Lovers can be friends too.' Then she gasped.

'What am I saying? That I expect more after this?'

His pride stepped up. 'Don't you want more?'

She rolled over so she could eyeball him. 'Aaron, we both know we've got our own futures sorted and they don't include us being together.'

'That wasn't my question.' Though he did want to know where she was going with this. 'But carry on.'

She surprised him. 'Making love with you was amazing. How's that for an answer? It's true, in case you think I'm trying to soothe your ego. I feel like I've been to the stars and back.'

His finger traced her lips. 'You know how to make me feel special.'

'As for your other question, I can't imagine I can let you walk away without making love to me again, but I am saying that I am not looking for anything permanent. I'm sure you understand why.'

'The baby? You don't think you can share your life once you're a parent?' A wave of sadness rolled over him. For Bella and himself.

Solo parents found partners all the time. Why not Bella?

'It's a lot to ask another man to take on Jason's child when I've deliberately got pregnant.' She looked sad. 'It's different from having been left with a child to raise alone.'

'Is it though? I guess some men might think you'll never get over losing Jason and they'd be competing for your love, but I'd say they'd be short on self-confidence.' If he fell in love with Bella and she reciprocated the feeling then he'd run with it, and never stop to look back. Because true love accepted *everything*. Except history had proved him wrong with Amy.

'You think?' She was smiling now, the sadness slowly taking a back seat.

If he'd made her happier, then he was glad to have helped. 'You know me well enough to understand if I say something I mean it. Or think it,' he added with a smile of his own. 'Now roll over and back in so I can cuddle you to sleep. You still look tired.'

'I wonder why.' Her smile stretched wide. 'But yes, I could do with some more Z's.'

Her firm butt pressed into his groin, making him horny as, but he resisted because Bella did need to catch up on sleep if she was going to function at all well in the morning. His arm slipped around her waist, her warm skin like silk against his palm. She relaxed against his chest as her breathing deepened and slowed.

Lying there, holding Bella, Aaron tried not to think too much about the future because really they didn't have one. As she'd pointed out, they had their own plans mapped out, which didn't include each other. Though that was getting harder by the day to accept. Nothing was fixed in concrete. He'd have to be an egotist not to be prepared to change anything to fit in with a woman he loved if that came about, and Bella was getting closer to his heart with every breath she took.

This was so cosy. Comfortable, mentally as well as physically. Something that had been missing for a long time, especially since the attack. His eyelids lifted and he stared over her shoulder at the far wall.

Under his arm Bella's chest rose and fell in soft movements. She was out to it. So trusting.

His eyes closed. He pushed them open. Breathed deep, long and hard. *Stay awake.*

Enjoy the warmth, the sharing, the trust. Shouting in his sleep would be a nightmare for them both. His breathing slowed along with his heart rate. So cosy.

The next thing Aaron knew he was opening his eyes and looking into Bella's steady gaze. 'Hello. Did I fall asleep?'

'You were out for the count when I woke about an hour ago.'

'You're kidding me.' He couldn't have been. He never slept more than a few minutes at a time.

'Why would I?' Then understanding dawned on her face. 'That attack haunts you at night.'

'Every night since it happened—until now. Unbelievable.' Even more unbelievable was how he was talking about it when he never mentioned it to anyone, not even his closest friends.

'You were comfortable with me.'

'True.' Could she stay every night from now on? Chance would be a fine thing. 'Or so completely relaxed after making love that nothing could intrude.' Not even a man with a knife.

'I know that feeling very well.' Her smile was infectious.

He laughed. 'Come here. Want some more comfort?'

'Can't think of a better way to start the day.' Her lips were heat on his mouth.

CHAPTER SIX

'JOHNNY'S AN ASTHMATIC,' Aaron told Bella. 'He presented with a serious headache on the right side. A migraine by my reckoning.'

Poor lad. 'Has he had them before?' Bella asked the distressed woman sitting by the bed.

'Never. He gets mild headaches during an asthma attack but nothing like this.'

'Johnny, what have you been doing today?'

'Swimming and riding my bike.'

'Did you fall off your bike? Bang your head on anything?'

'No, but there was a lot of glare on the water when I was swimming.'

'That could do it at a pinch.' Some people were more vulnerable than others. 'Do you do a lot of swimming?' she asked as a way of getting Johnny to relax. The tension wasn't helping his breathing and therefore his asthma attack was getting worse.

When he started gasping for air Aaron

handed him the oxygen mask. 'Put that on, and don't take it off this time.'

His mother took over. 'He swims as a way of expanding his lungs and keeping his breathing as normal as possible. But today he came home early because of his headache. Said it was really bad so I brought him here. Dr Aaron thought you should see him. Do you agree about the migraine? Johnny doesn't need any more problems.'

Bella nodded. 'I'm sure he doesn't, but Aaron's right. Johnny's suffering from a migraine, and since his asthma is flaring up I'd like to keep him in for a night to monitor his blood pressure and vitals to be sure it is a migraine and nothing else.'

Johnny stared at her. He was gasping for the oxygen and sweat had broken out on his forehead.

'I don't think there is another problem but I like to be certain. Anyway you need that oxygen at the moment. That's not a light asthma attack.' Bella looked to Aaron. 'Have you given him anything for the pain?'

He nodded and named the drug he'd prescribed. 'Johnny took it about twenty minutes ago so it should be kicking in by now.' Turning to their patient, he asked, 'Is the pain any better?'

Johnny held up his thumb and finger with a small gap between them.

'Good.'

'I know you're thirteen but I'm taking you to the children's ward. The general ward is full at the moment.' Bella gave a little laugh. 'You can be the boss of all the kids.'

He did an eye-roll, and tugged the mask to the side. 'Thanks a lot, Doc.'

'You're welcome.'

'He's spent enough nights in children's wards they feel like home to him,' Johnny's mother said.

'He has a lot of severe asthma attacks,' Aaron added.

She'd seen that in the notes. 'You're not locals or I'd have met you before.'

'Milan,' Aaron answered for Johnny. 'He's here for a school trip. His mother's a teacher's aide.'

Then he ended up in here. Her heart tugged for him. But to be fair, he wasn't behaving as if he'd been handed a raw deal. He was used to it and getting on with what needed to be done with the occasional grump. 'Are you having more or less attacks than you did as a child?'

This time his mother answered. 'No change really. Until today and the headache.'

'You haven't taken a tumble in the last day or two, have you?'

Johnny's eyes widened. He tugged the mask away. 'I fell off the bed yesterday.' Gasp. 'Me and another guy were horsing around.' Gasp. Deep inhale on the oxygen. 'I did knock my head but not hard and no headache.'

'But it might have started something.' Bella straightened up. 'Let's get you upstairs and I'll talk to your doctor back home.'

'Might be too late in the day for that,' Aaron pointed out. 'It's after six.'

No wonder her stomach was rumbling. Food was needed and the sooner the better. Her appetite had returned with a vengeance over the past couple of days. 'I'll give it a go anyway.'

'You were working late,' Aaron said as she headed to the desk and a phone.

'I've got a ten-year-old with leukaemia who returned from treatment in Milan about an hour ago. I like to make sure everything's going all right before I leave. I'll be keeping an eye on Johnny too.'

She glanced at Aaron and felt her heart swell. It was nearly a week since she'd spent the night in his bed. Far too long. They'd both been busy all week, her with extra appointments with patients from further afield, and Aaron on night shifts, so no catching up between his sheets. But she was also being cautious. Despite how much she wanted him, she was aware that whatever they'd started wasn't going anywhere long term. That made her wonder if she should call it quits before she was too involved, or if she should grab what was on offer and make the most of the time Aaron was in Stresa.

The thing was, he also seemed a little reluctant to rush into a full-on relationship. She didn't know why, but she couldn't argue with him because basically they were on the same page about not getting in too deep. She didn't know if he even wanted to see her again outside work. She thought he might, but wasn't certain. The man could do aloof very well. Add in the fact she wasn't used to getting into new relationships and it was a bit of a quagmire.

'I'll be around here if you happen to get

called in later.' His grin was wicked and did little to cool the need simmering in her veins.

Did that mean he might want some more time with her? She refused to overthink the answer. She'd already done six days on her own since they'd made love. She was starved for his company. 'Want me to bring in some spaghetti, by any chance?'

His eyes widened and his tongue did a lap of his lips. 'Yes, please, thank you, Doctor.'

She'd get Gino to put together two meals and join Aaron in the department tearoom. 'See you later.' Sounded like a promise, one she was glad to make. To hell with the future. Tonight she'd enjoy sharing a meal with Aaron amongst his calls to the ED.

'Delicious as usual. Gino's cooking would be as good a reason as any to apply for a permanent position here, if I didn't have a job back home.' Aaron pushed the plate aside and leaned back. Not quite as good as the one where he got to spend more time with Bella. If she was willing.

'I'll let him know.' She grinned. The grin disappeared as she became thoughtful.

'Maybe not?' Gino mightn't approve of him getting too close to his sister. He wouldn't want her being hurt again, though he did seem keen for her to find a partner so she wasn't raising her child alone.

Bella gave an exaggerated shrug. 'He likes the compliments as much as anybody.'

That was not what was putting the caution in her expression. 'Try again, Bella.' He was in the mood to push her a bit. They'd been relaxed around each other ever since making love. There hadn't been any talk of what came next, but neither had that caused tension whenever they'd caught up. If there was a problem between them, surely it would've been apparent? He knew he had to keep his distance when it came to his heart, but a little relaxation and fun didn't mean he was going all out to win her over.

Her sigh hung between them. 'Gino wants nothing more than for me to find a husband. He won't accept I'm not interested in another relationship. Not yet.' She was staring at her hands clenched together on the tabletop.

Okay, so he already knew this, but for some reason it hurt to hear it. Especially since they'd connected so well when they'd made love. Of course she was right, but that didn't make it any easier to accept. Pride? Probably. It was new for him to be turned away. Women flocked to him and it was usually him turning *them* away. Not that Bella was saying they'd have nothing to do with each other now, but still. He did have red blood in his veins and a big heart that needed filling. He shouldn't be thinking that. That was not up for grabs. Not until he was certain the woman he came to love could handle his lifestyle and background. He wasn't sure how Bella would cope with any of that. If she did keep it all in perspective, she'd probably still be worn down by all the hype eventually. He'd seen it before. Talk about jaded.

'Aaron? Have I gone too far?'

'No, I like your honesty. It leaves no doubts. More than that, I understand what you're saying.' Mostly, anyway, and not necessarily liking it, even if she was being honest, because it raised questions about his own reasons for staying single. Was he a coward? Should he take a chance? There was a lot to win, and a lot to lose. 'How about you tell him I thoroughly enjoyed dinner and that we are getting along fine without any expectations of a future together?'

Bella winced.

He'd touched a nerve. Who knew what that meant? She must have doubts about what she wanted looking ahead. Who didn't in situations like theirs? He wasn't asking for another round of honesty just yet. It was painful for both of them. Leaning forward, he covered those tight fists balled in her lap.

'Bella, it's all right. You and I know where we stand with each other.' Did they though? 'That's all that matters. As you've pointed out, we have our futures planned and they don't include each other beyond whatever happens over the next few months.' He hated saying that, but he was supporting her, and repeating what he'd agreed to. 'It has nothing to do with your brother.' Gino knew Aaron would never deliberately hurt his sister. That was what mattered here.

A nurse appeared in the doorway. 'Aaron, you're needed. An elderly man's had cardiac arrest and the ambulance is only minutes away.'

'Coming.' He stood up and reached for the dirty plates.

'I'll look after those,' Bella told him. 'Then I'll check on my patients before heading home.' She looked a bit woebegone.

'Bella, don't overthink everything.'

'Actually, I was going to say let's go for a walk tomorrow afternoon once you've caught up on some sleep, but I shouldn't be walking too much and you like to get out amongst it.'

Knock me down. Now I'm really confused.

So, he'd go with what he'd honestly like to do. 'Here's another idea. I could take the chair-lift from this side to the top of the hill and hike down into Orta and meet you there for a late lunch.' He did like to stride out hard and fast. Over the past few weeks he'd come to realise how much the hiking was rejuvenating him physically and, more importantly, mentally. Though some of the mental improvement he put down to time spent with Bella.

Her hair fell across her cheek when she nodded. 'Agreed. I can go for a small stroll by the lake and pretend I'm being physically active.' She wasn't happy about staying off her feet as much as possible, but he knew how determined she was to keep this baby so she was taking it seriously.

'Decision made. I'll set my alarm for eleven in the morning. I'm not rostered on tomorrow night.'

'I'll drive you back to your apartment afterwards.'

He didn't bother arguing. It didn't matter who was behind the wheel. Only who he was with, and Bella was his pick.

So much for keeping his distance. He'd get back on track next week.

Which meant he had no hang-ups about making love to Bella when they got back to his apartment. Nor could he stop smiling when she curled into him and said she'd like to stay the night with him. More hugs, cuddles, kisses and love making eventuated, making him happier than he could ever remember being.

Hard to put up the barriers after that and the following days were filled with more of the same.

The next week Bella blew his socks off once more. 'It's my parents' wedding anniversary in a couple of weeks and we're having a family day out on Isola Bella. Would you like to join us?' she asked when they crossed paths in the hospital. 'The restaurant owners are friends of Gino's and they're organising everything, even the catering.'

Aaron laughed. 'Bet that's got Gino in a lather. He does like to be in control of the food.'

'Believe me, Micco is in charge. They go way back and Gino knows when to behave.'

'This should be interesting. As for your invitation, I'd love to come. Are you sure your parents won't mind?'

'It was Papà's idea, though I had already been going to ask you.' Bella's mouth twitched. 'My family seem to have taken a shine to you.'

'I'd better be on my best behaviour, then.'

'Why spoil things?' Bella grinned.

His stomach knotted with desire. She could turn him on with nothing more than a glance, so a cheeky grin was like adding fire to dynamite. 'That's the last thing I want to do.' He felt the note of caution in his words, and hoped Bella hadn't.

Isola Bella was a popular tourist attraction, which raised caution. Back home, whenever he went to a function, the first thing he thought about was how to avoid the media. Here, where he could still walk around town freely, he hadn't had to do that yet. The last thing he wanted was anyone with a microphone or camera turning up to ask him about the people he was keeping company with. So far he'd escaped attention in Stresa, but old habits didn't die overnight. Long may that last. He knew no matter how hard he tried to stay in the background, it was impossible if the media wanted to know what he was up to.

'You've gone quiet on me.'

He shook his head abruptly. 'Didn't mean to. Tell me where I meet you all and I'll make sure I'm there on time.' Without any nosey followers.

'Come around to my apartment and we'll go from there. We'll probably have a carload of excited kids to cope with.' She laughed. 'Hope you're up for that.'

'Totally inexperienced but happy to give it my all.'

'No nieces or nephews?'

'My sister isn't in a relationship; too focused on her career. I doubt whether she'll ever settle down enough to have a family.' Kind of sad, but then he wasn't sure if the opportunity would arise for him either for different reasons.

Having kids of his own with the right woman would be wonderful. His eyes flicked to Bella.

She would be the right woman. She'd be a fantastic wife. And she was going to be a wonderful mother.

Yeah, and you're so not ready for that.

But he was thinking about it more often these days. Not so long ago thinking like that about a woman would never have occurred to him. Bella had him warming to the idea of taking another chance on love.

Bella nudged him in the side. 'You're doing it again.' A stern look came his way. 'If you'd prefer not to come, just say so.'

'You couldn't be further from the truth. I can't wait to spend time with you, and your family since they're so accepting of me.'

'Why wouldn't they be?'

If only she knew. No, he didn't want her finding out about his lifestyle back home. Not yet. There was no avoiding the day when he had to tell her, but he wanted to make the most of the time he had with her uninterrupted by nosey parkers thinking he owed the world something. He faked a shrug. 'Who knows? You're their daughter and sister. They might be picky about who you see.'

'You're failing to convince me that you're being completely honest here, Aaron.'

Fair enough. 'I'm not used to being accepted without lots of questions about my future and what I want.' It was true, in a roundabout way.

'Why would that be?'

No getting off lightly. 'This is bigger than a two-minute discussion in the hospital hallway. Can we defer it till another time?'

Bella leaned back against the wall, her hand on her baby bump. 'Are you avoiding something?'

Absolutely. Who wouldn't if it meant curtailing what was turning out to be the best experience he'd had in years? 'I have been, but you're right, the time has come to talk to you.' Two nurses walked past, laughing over something one had said. 'Not here though.'

A phone rang. Not his.

Bella looked disgruntled when she realised it was hers. 'Saved by the phone, eh?' Pressing the phone to her ear, she answered, 'Dr Bella Rosso.'

It would be too easy to walk away while

he could, but he wasn't a coward. He might loathe the hype that surrounded his family but he wasn't about to turn his back on Bella when she'd been so understanding about his nightmares over the attack.

'I've got to go. That was a pathologist from Milan. Haematology's back on a two-year-old boy. Acute myeloid leukaemia.' Her shoulders sank in on themselves as her face darkened. 'I hate these moments. Now I'm going to be a *mamma* it's even worse, if that's possible.'

Aaron placed a hand on her shoulder. 'Breathe, Bella. In, out. That's it. You've got this.'

For a long minute they stood like that, then she straightened, drew a deep breath and gave him a crooked smile. 'You make me feel I can do anything. I'll see you later?'

'Yes.' Whether to discuss his family or her afternoon that was about to unfold he had no idea. Possibly both, but he'd be there for Bella. No way he wouldn't be. 'You can count on it.'

'Thought I might be able to.'

Or should I have said, I was afraid to trust him not to let me down? Bella pondered as she headed for the children's ward and the nightmare waiting there. She preferred thinking about Aaron's hesitancy and what it might mean to their growing friendship than facing what she now had to tell Nigel's parents. Yet he'd been quick to touch her with that tenderness he seemed to keep bottled inside. He understood how tough this was for her.

'Put your big girl's pants on,' she admonished herself. This wasn't the first time she'd had to deliver heartbreaking news to parents, nor would it be the last. It still didn't make things any easier. Her hand did a circle of her baby bump. Doing something like this was even more real. Being a parent made a person vulnerable.

'The file's on screen for you,' Gita told her as she swept into the office, trying to look more confident than she felt.

'There's a bed reserved at Milan Hospital for Nigel. We need to arrange a transfer asap.'

'I'll get onto it right away.'

Dropping onto the hard chair, Bella swiped the screen and tapped 'open', then proceeded to read all the data the pathologist had summarised over the phone. It didn't make pleasant reading, even when she'd been warned about what to expect. Finally she stood up and, holding her head high, went to talk to her patient's parents.

'I'm shattered,' Bella told Aaron later that night as they sat on his veranda and watched the sun sink behind the Alps. 'Explaining the leukaemia to Nigel's parents was hard work. They're struggling to believe it, as has every parent I've ever told something similar to. I can't begin to imagine what it must be like.' Both her hands were on her stomach, protecting Sophia from all the horrors out in the real world.

'Here, get this into you.' Aaron placed a mug of green tea on the small table by her chair. 'My landlady swears it's the best thing for stress.'

'Better than wine?' Which she wasn't having while she was pregnant.

'Probably not, but we're behaving.' He sank onto a chair beside her and reached over to rub between her shoulders.

How did he know there was a tight knot there that ached whichever way she held herself? 'That's good,' she murmured, sipping the tea. 'The tea's not too bad either.'

'Want to talk?'

'Nigel's on his way to hospital in Milan as we speak. His mum's with him and dad's following in the car. The grandparents are looking after their other son, who's five.' Another sip of tea. 'The pathologist is going to take a bone-marrow sample first thing tomorrow morning. Then he'll start treatment as soon as he's read the smears.' She shivered. 'That's it, really. Acute leukaemia can have a good outcome in young children but the treatment's harsh.' She would not cry. She wouldn't.

'Here, take a handful.' Aaron passed her a box of tissues.

Maybe a few tears were allowed. 'I'm the kid's doctor. I'm not supposed to cry.'

'You're also human. It would be odd if you didn't get tearful. Hell, I feel a bit that way and I've had nothing to do with your patient or his parents.'

She reached for his hand, because he made her feel better without any falsehood. A genuine guy through and through. 'The downside to being a doctor, isn't it? It's even harder in this case because I know the family. Jenny grew up in the same street as me, though she's a couple of years younger, and we were best buddies.'

'She hoped you'd perform miracles when you mentioned why you'd ordered haematology tests?'

'You're onto it. Though I didn't mention leukaemia, I did say Nigel looked very anaemic, which went with his lethargy. Then there are all the bruises covering his body. Jenny's no slug. She cottoned on to the fact I was thinking something more than a minor illness.'

'Why didn't you hand Nigel over to someone else?'

'Who? It's a small town. Everyone knows everyone. One of the other specialists at the practice isn't a local but he's away on leave this week. Besides, it's probably nicer for Jenny and Geo that they know me.'

'Fair enough.'

Baby kicked. Bella gasped, and placed her hand on the spot. 'Wow. Are you going to be a footballer, my girl?'

'Baby's letting you know she's awake?'

'Do you want to feel her kick?' She held her breath. Was that going too far? Probably. This baby had nothing to do with Aaron, and, while he was very supportive of her, it didn't mean he wanted to get too close.

‘Can I?’ he asked. ‘I’d love to.’

‘Give me your hand.’ She placed his palm on her abdomen, refusing to think about what might be going on in his mind. ‘Just wait. There. Feel that?’

The look of wonder in his eyes told her yes.

‘Wow. That’s amazing. I’ve never known that before. Well, not quite true. When I was training there was a six-month-pregnant woman in our class who let everyone touch the spot where her baby was moving, but that was impersonal. This…’ He paused and looked at Bella. ‘This feels different. I’ve held your body. Made love to you, and now to feel your baby move is wonderful.’

Blow her over. When the man put his soul into it, he could say the most heart-rending things. ‘That’s how I felt the first time Sophia moved, and I have every time since. It’s like she’s telling me she’s in there and I’d better not ignore her. I never understood how intense being pregnant could be, and I should have. I’ve heard plenty of women say the same thing, but I guess when it came to me I believed being a doctor would take some of the gloss away.’

'It hasn't, has it? I'm stunned and I'm not the one carrying the baby.'

Nor was he the father. That was what he was really saying. Which kind of saddened her. He'd be a great dad. Talk about getting ahead of herself. They were friends who'd become lovers. Best not to hurry and find out what lay ahead, and instead make the most of what they had together. One day at a time, she reminded herself.

She was still in the dark about how far she wanted this to go. Aaron ticked a lot of boxes, but when she'd decided to become pregnant with Jason's child she'd planned on going it alone. To bring Aaron into the picture needed a lot of consideration from all aspects. He had to be one hundred per cent on board, and they were nowhere near that with a lot to share about their pasts and what they wanted further ahead. It was quite possible they'd never be that close. She went with light-hearted because to get too deep wasn't a good idea at the moment.

'Men get the easy job when it comes to babies.' She laughed.

'I reckon. But then there are all the years that follow, and dads are very involved then.'

'You would be. I know that for sure.'

'Thank you for the vote of confidence.' He looked pleased.

Didn't he get many compliments? When everyone at the hospital thought he was a superb doctor? When her family believed he was a genuine man who wanted nothing more than to be a part of everything going on? When he had her back even before he got to know her? 'I could go on but then your head might get too big to hold up.'

He leaned back in his chair and sipped his beer. 'You know something? I haven't been so relaxed with a woman in for ever.'

'Why not?'

'You don't want so much from me that I forget why I liked you in the first place.'

There was more to that than first seemed likely, but right now she wasn't about to dig deep. The tension brought on by Nigel's diagnosis was slipping away and she was feeling comfortable again. All due to this man. No need to spoil the moment. Turning to him, she leaned close and kissed him. Lightly, softly. Her heart squeezed. He was just who she needed right now. Pressing harder, she kissed deeper, slipping her tongue into his mouth and savouring his heat.

'Bella,' he groaned under her mouth.

She pulled back enough to say, 'What I want right now is for us to make love.'

He took her face in his hands and locked his eyes on her. 'I'd like that very much.'

What could be better?

Later, as they lay in Aaron's bed, holding hands, Bella stared at the ceiling and said quietly, 'Tell me some more about your family.' More? She knew nothing.

His hand stiffened. Then he withdrew it. 'What would you like to know?'

So he was putting it back on her. Avoiding something? 'You've said my lot are close and all encompassing, unlike yours. Why are they so different?'

Silence. The frown on his brow suggested he was thinking about where to go with this.

She waited patiently. Forcing Aaron to talk might cause distress, but at the same time she wanted to get to know him better. Needed to if they were to stay together for longer than a fling.

He rolled onto his side, his head on his hand. Looking at her, he sighed. 'My parents have always been deeply involved in their careers. To the point the careers came before me and my sister.'

How could any parent do that? 'That must've been hard.'

'It was. My sister's much the same now, though at least she understands it wouldn't be wise to have children and then treat them the same way we were.'

'What does she do?'

'She works in the film industry as a camera operator. A very good one, at that.'

'Being very good must run in the family as her brother's an exceptional emergency doctor, by all accounts.'

His smile was tight. 'Thanks.' He huffed out a breath. 'My father is a high court judge and my mother is a well-known actress. They make the headlines often, including my sister. While I'm happy for them all, the hype that goes with that is mind-boggling at times and drives me crazy. There's no such thing as privacy for any of us.'

'Even you?'

'Even me.' He was watching her intently. 'My family's wealthy, which only adds to the media circus. They seem to think they have the right to ask personal questions and get abusive when I don't give them the answers they want. When I was young I thought it was normal and fine, but out in the real world I began to understand what it was like for other people living quieter, less fortunate lives. Strange as it sounds, I wanted that.'

'You'd like the family life I grew up in?'

'Absolutely. I'm used to being followed and hassled by media, but there're times when they interfere in my private life too much. It affects relationships and friendships in ways I don't like.'

'I can imagine.'

'I doubt it. Though I also believe you wouldn't like the attention either.'

'I'd hate it. I had a couple of encounters with the media when Jason hit the headlines over a life-changing medical technique he developed.' The reporters had wanted to know all about her, which was so irrelevant. No one had the right to shove a camera in anyone's face so they could get a story to titillate the readers and probably be forgotten by breakfast time the next day. 'Was the attack on you in ED made into a big deal because of who you are?'

'Yes.' He rolled onto his back. 'The thing is, that attack would've made headline news no matter who the victim was. It was horrendous. But because Aaron Marshall was nearly killed the stories went on for ever, making it hard to go into work and carry on as though nothing had happened. It seemed as though every patient wanted me to be their doctor so they could say they'd been treated by someone famous.'

Bella felt her heart expand for this man who had been hurt physically and mentally by a crazed person. Also by his family, if she was reading him right. Moving closer, she wrapped her arms around him and held him tight. 'You're awesome.'

He stiffened. 'You think?'

'I do. I can't begin to imagine what you've been through. But you're here, carrying on as though nothing happened while looking out for others. It's your nature to be a caring doctor and nothing's changed in that respect because of what happened.'

The tension eased out of him. He placed his

hand on her back, his fingers making light circles on her skin. 'You're different from any woman I've been close to before, Bella. Thank you.'

For what? Being herself? That could be the case. Fame brought its own problems. She kissed his chest, then tongued his nipple, and felt him hardening against her. What better way to move on from his telling her about his life, albeit nothing too deep, and be able to let go the tension completely?

Reaching between them, she took him in her hand and began to make him harder.

CHAPTER SEVEN

'HAPPY ANNIVERSARY, Angela and Marco. Forty years and still counting.' Aaron handed Bella's mother the gift he'd bought them.

'Grazie.' Angela leaned in and brushed a kiss on his cheek. 'You didn't have to buy us anything. Enjoying the celebrations with our family is enough.'

'Maybe, but I wanted to get you something special.' He'd spent his day off during the week in Milan, taking in some of the sights, and when he'd walked past a shop with handcrafted wooden artwork in the window he'd stepped inside. Blown away by the beauty of some of the pieces, he'd known the bowl he kept returning to touch would be the right present for this lovely couple. They had a couple of pieces on the counter in the restaurant that he'd twice seen Angela caress as she walked by.

This family was coming to mean something special to him. Not only because of Bella, but because of how they accepted him into their midst without question. That was such a new experience he couldn't resist even though he knew it might bring trouble to their door if he got too involved. It was almost guaranteed the day would come when the media would learn where he was and who he was dating. Reporters seemed to be born with extra-sensory noses for trouble.

'It's beautiful. *Grazie*, Aaron,' Angela said.

Bella came to stand beside him. 'It's just the sort of thing Mamma loves.'

Glad he'd got it right, he gave her a smile. He'd been doing that a lot since he'd told her about his family. 'Thank goodness I followed my gut instinct.'

Bella hadn't overreacted or asked more questions about the wealth or fame that made life difficult for the Marshall clan. Basically she'd accepted what he'd told her and continued on as though it didn't matter. She might be a good actress but he didn't think that was the case. They'd shared his bed twice since and she'd been as enthusiastic as ever without appearing to be trying to inveigle her way into his heart. Yes, he was being cynical, but that came with the territory. Though if he wanted a real life that included a woman and children it was time to move on from that.

'Come and meet some more family.'

When he winced she laughed.

'I'm Italian. There're a lot of aunts and uncles and therefore cousins.'

'You're saying you all have large families?'

She grinned. 'I intend having at least six kids.'

The crazy thing was he could see her surrounded by that many, all laughing and demanding attention—which they'd get, along with lots of love. 'One at a time, eh?'

'Realistically, probably only this one.' Her hand did his favourite circle thing on her stomach.

Then he really heard what she'd said. 'You don't intend having more?'

'None that are in the plan at the moment, but—' Her shrug was eloquent. 'Who knows what lies ahead? I'm not racing to unravel the future. One step—one baby—at a time.'

'Fair enough.' Hopefully she also meant she was open to a different man in her life for the next one. If he was her pick, that was. Because no matter how hard he was trying to deny he cared a lot for her, he was well along the path to being in love with her.

'Come on. Let's stop being serious. This is supposed to be a happy day.' Taking his hand, she led him across to a group of people leaning over the balustrade facing out over the lake. 'Hey, everyone, I'd like you to meet Aaron. He's relieving in Stresa's emergency department. He's also a special friend of mine.'

Special, eh? He'd take that for now. 'Hi. I'll try to remember all your names.'

'These are my brothers. Elio has an IT business based here, and Marco works in Roma.'

He shook hands with the men and received kisses on his cheeks from the women, along with a few studied looks from the brothers. Did he make the grade? He hoped so.

'Aaron, there you are. I need some help.' Gino appeared from the building.

'Whatever with?'

'Salmon. You're a Scotsman, you must know the best way to cook one.'

'I thought you had the day off from the kitchen.'

'*Sì*, and you'd walk away from someone

needing your medical help because you were at a party?' Gino laughed. 'Come with me.'

'Cooking's not my forte.'

'What's the best meal of salmon you've ever had? That's what I want to know.'

'Have you got some honey?'

'Sì.'

'Garlic and lemon?'

'You're in Italy, man. What do you think?'

Hadn't he said cooking wasn't his thing? 'Right, let's go.'

Inside the kitchen, Gino handed Aaron a beer. 'Tell me, is Bella over whatever made her so tired last month?'

Ah ha. Away from his sister, Gino wanted info. 'She isn't so exhausted, and is trying to take it easy. Or at least be less physical than usual.' Other than in his bed, where she was very energetic.

'That's what she told me, almost word for word.'

'Then believe her.' Aaron wasn't about to go into detail about Bella's pregnancy worries. It wasn't his place, and wouldn't earn him any points if she found out.

'I do. Because she told me that there's been

some spotting and she's being extra careful now. She also said it is quite normal, but she's taking it as a warning not to overdo anything.'

Relief filled Aaron that Gino knew. 'That's also true.'

Gino thumped him on the back. 'I like you. You're discreet. I think you care about my sister.'

How discreet did the man want him to be? 'I do.'

That's all I'm saying.

'About the salmon?'

'Under control. But I do like the honey, garlic and lemon idea too. Come on, there's another salmon in the chiller. Let's see what we can do to that one. You go and keep my sister happy.'

'Yes, sir.' He grinned, his heart as light as air.

From the patio Bella watched Aaron kneel down to tie a shoelace for one of the boys, and smiled to herself. He was quite at ease with everyone.

From the little he'd told her about growing up, being so comfortable around her family wouldn't come easily. Hard to imagine not having his parents there to talk and play when he needed them. To be sent to boarding school at the age of ten seemed cruel. Why have children if you weren't going to be a part of their growing up and see them change daily? It was unfathomable, and not the kind of parent she'd be. Sure, she still intended working, but not every hour of every day. She wanted to be there for and with her daughter.

'You're smitten.' Cara stood beside her, a glass of wine in hand.

'Not sure that's a good thing.' Bella felt a pang of love for Aaron. 'I'm carrying Jason's baby. It'd be a big ask for Aaron to accept that. I'm not sure I'm ready either. We're not so involved to be discussing a future together,' she added hurriedly.

Her sister-in-law might've guessed she was keen on Aaron, but she didn't need to know how much. Next thing the whole family would be at her to grab him while she could. They really longed for her to find another man and settle down again, but they also had to understand she had to be ready. As much as she was falling for Aaron, taking that last step and admitting her love would be huge. There'd be no turning back if she did, so she had to be certain it was the right move—especially for her daughter.

'Don't go making problems if there aren't any,' Cara warned.

'Good point.'

'Did you and Jason discuss you marrying again?'

They'd brushed over the topic but as it had made her uncomfortable they'd moved on fast. 'Not really.' Though Jason had said she was not to remain single for ever, that she deserved a second chance. She just wasn't sure if and when she might be ready for such a commitment, but if the way her heart went into overdrive when Aaron was around was anything to go by she was inching nearer.

'He's a good-looking dude.' Cara laughed.

'I'm not denying that.'

'Bella, take your time. We're all here for you and will support you no matter what goes down.'

'I know, and I'm very grateful. Family is everything, isn't it?' Something she'd like to give Aaron. She took a good look at that lithe body strolling towards her. Those firm thighs and that strong chest turned her on in a blink, and had her wanting to kiss him until she was senseless with passion. Yes, he was becoming more than a friend with benefits, way more.

The nights she spent in his apartment were the best she'd known in a while. He made her feel cared about in a way that was personal, deep and meaningful. A lot like how Jason had loved her. Dared she admit that? Hard not to when it was the truth. But she wasn't comparing. Not really. As far as personalities went, the two men who had inched into her heart were poles apart.

Jason was louder, more out there, and had fully expected her to follow his lead in a lot of their lifestyle decisions. Of course, she'd stood up to him on numerous occasions, and he'd once admitted he'd have been disappointed if she hadn't, that her strength was one thing he loved about her. His career had been just as important to him as Aaron's was, but he'd also made sure everyone knew how good he was.

Quite the opposite to Aaron, who was exceptional and put his patients before his ego. Jason had loved her so much that she'd always felt special. She suspected Aaron would be the same if he were to fall for her. He always had her back, even around her family where it wasn't really needed but appreciated just the same.

'Catch, Zia Bella.'

A ball flew past her head. She resisted spinning around to snatch at it. Baby had only just settled down from a long kicking match of her own and no way did Bella want to shake her out of her quiet time. 'Catch it yourself.' She laughed at her nephew.

'Do they ever run out of energy?' Aaron asked as he joined her.

'Not very often.' She glanced up at him. 'You're looking very relaxed. Sleep well last night?'

'Only woke once and that wasn't because of a nightmare. I seem to finally be moving on from those a little.'

'I'm glad.' It must be hell having a rerun of that hideous attack every night.

He brushed a kiss on her cheek. 'You have a lot to do with it. All the walking I'm doing is good for me too. I start out feeling average and by the time I'm done I feel on top of the world.'

'The exercise will help you sleep better too.' He didn't go for strolls—unless with her—but seemed to hike hard and fast up in the hills or around the lake.

'Stresa has a lot going for it.' He grinned.

'There's a position coming up later in the year.' It'd be wonderful if he moved here permanently.

Hold on, Bella. That would mean opening up and becoming serious about your feelings for him.

Maybe that was the nudge she needed to move forward, to start a new life with another loving man. A big step. She never used to be afraid of taking those. That had been before she'd known how fast and hard the rug could be pulled out from under her and leave her in a heap on the ground, which was not an excuse to hide from life. She just hadn't thought she might get to be so lucky twice. Not that she knew if that was the case with Aaron yet. Too soon, too confronting maybe.

Looking at him, she added, 'Think about it. But don't wait for ever. Someone else might beat you to it.'

He nodded. 'Management mentioned it last week. I'll consider it, but there's still my job back home. I also think I'd miss the intensity of the larger EDs long term.'

Swallowing the disappointment that brought on, she said, 'Your call.' No wonder she was trying hard not to rush into anything too serious with him.

'If I decide to move here, I need to be certain it's the right thing to do. It would mean letting down the people at Edinburgh Hospital who've supported me so much, and…' He paused, looking at her intently. 'I don't want to take advantage of us, and you, and how well we're getting on. I would prefer to see where we're going first.'

Her heart stuttered. He was getting serious about her and them. He was also being cautious and considerate. She could go with that. 'You're amazing.' Leaning in, she kissed him.

His mouth opened under hers and he kissed her back before withdrawing. 'We need to be a little circumspect.'

'True.' She sighed. For once she wanted to let go and forget how her family would be coming up with any number of ideas about where this was headed.

Aaron laughed. 'One day at a time, remember?'

Had they really agreed to that? 'I hate it when you're right.'

'Sometimes I do too,' he agreed with a wicked glint in his eyes. 'Let's go and join the adults and keep our feet firmly on the ground.'

'What are you doing tonight?' she asked as they strolled around the side of the building to the lawn sweeping down to the lake edge.

'Hopefully taking a certain paediatrician home and having my way with her sexy body. Oh, and her mind,' he added cheekily.

Taking his hand in hers, she smiled. 'I'll be there.'

'I think we've got an audience.'

Looking around at everyone sitting under the awning stretched over the lawn, she felt a wave of happiness roll through her. Her family were watching them with nothing but acceptance on their faces. 'I could say let's give them a show, but better not.'

'No, thanks.'

Yes, please.

Aaron longed to sweep Bella up into his arms and rush away to somewhere quiet and private so he could kiss her blind. With her family watching on that wasn't happening. Instead he'd go with enjoying the day and this wonderful family who seemed to accept him for who he was and nothing more or less.

That alone was wonderful, and so new. Of course, they knew nothing about him outside Stresa. Not one of them could've looked him up on the Internet or he'd know. There'd be some look or question that'd have alerted him. Especially from Gino. He knew the signs all too well not to recognise when a person was digging into his background. Today he was a part of the gathering to celebrate Angela and Marco's wedding anniversary, and he felt good. So good it had him wondering if he *could* move here permanently. To be with Bella and her baby, to have a real family life and a future with this wonderful woman. Forty years of their own?

'Stop thinking too much.' Bella nudged him. 'Just go with the day and what it has to offer.'

It scared him how well she read him. 'Yes, ma'am. What can I get you to drink?'

'Sparkling water with a squeeze of lemon.'

It was late by the time they made it back to the apartment. The celebrations had gone on long after the enormous meal with endless toasts to the happy couple. 'That was a fantastic day,' Aaron told Bella as they settled on his deck with mugs of tea in hand. 'I'm glad you invited me.'

'Any time,' she replied. 'It can be a bit overwhelming if you're not used to so many people crowding around and acting like they've always known you. I know Jason found it daunting the first time he came to my family events. It's the Italian way, I suppose.'

'I like it.' More than liked it.

'Which reminds me, I'm heading across to London in a week to see Jason's parents.' Her shoulders rose and fell. 'It's something I'm going to do every couple of months so they don't feel I'm leaving them out of the pregnancy. They are my baby's grandparents and deserve to be kept in the picture. Literally, as I will take a copy of that scan for them to see.'

'You're not close?'

'Not the same as my family, but Jason's family have always been a bit more remote. They've supported me having this baby though, so I will support them in whatever they're doing.' There wasn't a lot of enthusiasm in her voice.

'I think they worry I'll fade out of their lives, taking Sophia away from them, but I'd never do that.'

'Will you stay with them?' His sister kept emailing to ask when he was going to go visit her. Something about catching up before she headed to the States at the end of July, where she would be working on a film for the rest of the year.

He could go over to London the same weekend as Bella and spend some time with her when she wasn't tied up with Jason's family, but that made him uncomfortable. He wasn't ready for the repercussions if the media saw them together. Eventually they'd have to face it if they were going to continue in this relationship but right now the idea of exposing Bella to all the hype and finding she wanted out didn't sit well. Of course, sooner rather than later was the best option and then he'd know where he stood, but the thought of losing Bella made him tight in the belly. No way. The idea chilled his skin. She was wonderful.

'I'll stay a night with them and then head home, unless you wanted to meet up for a night somewhere afterwards.' Again she'd read his mind too easily.

Sweat broke out between his shoulder blades. She seemed to be in agreement when it came to spending time together. But for him a night in London was another step forward and he wasn't sure he should be taking it. Was this make-or-break time?

'I'd prefer to stay here and share the night with you when you return. When I came to Stresa I decided I wasn't going back to Britain until my four months were up.' It was true. 'I wanted a complete change and to immerse myself in Italy as I tried to get past what kept me awake at night.'

'Fair enough. It could've been fun getting away together, that's all. We seem to be getting along so well sometimes I forget we've agreed there is no future together.' Heat spread across her face.

'Does that bother you?'

'A little.' She swallowed hard. 'I don't usually speak my mind so freely. Well…' Her blush deepened. 'I haven't exactly come out with startling news but it's more than I've said about my feelings for a long time.'

'To think when I first saw you at that car-versus-cycle accident I thought you were aloof.'

'I didn't want you thinking I might fancy you.'

'Did you? Then?'

'Not a lot. I was trying very hard not to anyway.' Suddenly she laughed. 'This is a crazy conversation.' She drained her mug and stood up. 'Take me to bed, will you?' Then she winced and her hand instantly covered her baby bump.

'Bella? What's wrong?'

She huffed out a breath. 'A sharp twinge. That's all.' Her eyes were wide as she stared down to where baby Sophia lay.

'Easy does it. Sit down.' Holding her elbow, he pressed her gently back onto the chair she'd just vacated. 'How sharp was the twinge?'

'Four out of ten.'

'This isn't a time to downplay the level of pain.'

Her worried eyes locked on him. 'If anything I'm exaggerating. I do not want anything going wrong with this pregnancy.'

'Fair enough. Anything more going on? Pain anywhere else?' He was in emergency-doctor mode, only it was difficult when the patient was Bella. Instinct told him to wrap her up in cotton wool and protect her and baby.

'No.' She was holding her breath, definitely waiting for something more to happen. Another stab of pain in her abdomen, or in her back? Or even a contraction?

'Bella, look at me.' He held her hands firmly and waited for her to raise her head. The worry in her eyes nearly undid him. She was terrified something was about to go horribly wrong, and if it did what were the chances he could prevent it? 'Hold onto me. Lean into me. Breathe evenly and regularly. It's been a busy day and you're tired. This could be a reaction to that. Twinges during pregnancy are not uncommon.' They'd dealt with this only weeks ago.

'I know. On one side of my brain anyway, but the other side's doing panic circles. I can't lose Sophia now. She's real, especially now I've seen her and named her. Why did I do that? It was tempting fate.'

Her lips were chilly when he kissed them lightly. 'You did what the majority of would-be parents do. You fell deeper in love with your baby and naming her brought her closer. It does not mean she's in trouble.'

She hadn't had another twinge unless she was hiding it from him, and he doubted that. Her expression was all about worry and fear but nothing sudden or sharp had deepened it. 'You're doing fine.'

'You think?'

He couldn't answer yes and later be proven wrong. 'I think you should go to bed and get some rest. I'll take your BP for peace of mind but, as that hasn't been an issue so far, I can't see that being the cause for a twinge of pain. But first how about you check for spotting?'

Fear appeared in her face.

'You know it's the right thing to do and most likely will ease your mind a little if there's nothing there. I'll also check your abdomen once you're in bed, if that's all right?'

'You're so patient with me.'

'Why wouldn't I be? Apart from it being my normal doctor approach, I care too much about you, and therefore your baby, to be anything else. I've got your back, Bella.'

'Don't I know it? Fine, I'll be the sensible patient and lie down so you can make certain everything's in place.'

He put on his stern voice. 'After you've looked for bleeding.'

Her smile was tight but it was real. 'Of course.'

No spotting, and everything seemed to be in the right place in Bella's abdomen. No more twinges either. He breathed in relief. Shrugging out of his clothes, Aaron climbed into bed and wrapped his arm over her waist. 'Go to sleep. I'll be here all night.'

Twisting over onto her side, she kissed him. 'You make sure you get some sleep too.'

'Only once you've shown me how.' He kissed her back, a kiss filled with care and love. He wanted this pregnancy to work out for Bella almost as much as she did.

'I'll do my best.'

'Then baby has nothing to worry about.'

When she rolled onto her other side he spooned behind her and held her throughout the night, sleep not coming his way once.

'I look like I've climbed the Alps overnight. The swelling under my eyes is terrible.' Bella regarded the image staring back at her from Aaron's bathroom mirror. 'My patients are going to run when they see me.'

'Sure you don't want to take the day off?' he asked as he picked up his shaver.

'No, I'm good to go. Tired and looking awful, but otherwise all good. I won't go rushing around like a demented cat, but sitting around home doing absolutely nothing would drive me insane and have me imagining all sorts of things going wrong with Sophia.'

'I get that. Have you got a full workload today?'

She nodded. 'From what I saw on Friday it's going to be busy but I'll manage.' She wasn't turning into a wimp no matter how important this pregnancy was to her. Being weak wouldn't help the baby, nor her own mind.

'No surprise there.'

She watched as he shaved, the passion that had taken a back seat last night suddenly rushing to the fore. Aaron was unbelievably hot. That firm jawline turned her on, as did his naked body. If only they had time to get down and sexy before heading out to work, but Aaron was due in the emergency department in forty minutes and she needed to get home for some fresh clothes and breakfast before heading to the paediatric centre. Forgoing breakfast was possible despite feeling starving hungry, but yesterday's clothes definitely needed changing. It might be time to carry a small bag in the car with spare gear in it.

'Are you going to work full-time right through to the end of your pregnancy?' Aaron asked.

'No. Luna's going to take on some of my hours in the third trimester.' Her partners, Luna and Alberto, were going to share the ED calls and her patients who came back for repeat visits. She'd talk to Luna later today and explain how tired she was getting and about the twinges to pre-warn her that she might have to step up earlier than planned.

'I'm glad you've got that in place. I had an awful thought you might work right through to the last moment.' He wasn't joking if the severe look on his face was an indicator.

'I am not taking any risks, which means cutting back my hours as I see fit.' Did he think she'd be irresponsible? If so then he didn't know her at all, and she was certain he had come to understand how important this baby was to her.

He held his hand up in a stop sign. 'I didn't mean to sound so harsh but I know how worried you are about seeing this through to the end safely. I was only adding my two euros' worth. I don't want anything going wrong either.'

Swallowing her ire, she nodded. She was more sensitive to criticism these days. 'Take no notice of me. I get a bit wound up at times. Right, I'll see you later.' She stretched up and brushed a kiss on his newly shaven chin. 'Hopefully not in ED.' Though she did like working with him, she didn't need young patients being admitted just so as she could see him.

'I agree.' He didn't return her kiss, and his smile appeared a little remote.

'Problem?'

He shook his head. 'No, but I'd better get a move on. The time is ticking by and I'm due on duty soon.'

You could still give me a smile.

She shrugged. 'I won't hold you up any longer.' Only minutes before he'd been acting as though he had all the time in the world. 'Bye.' She'd even wanted to return to his bed. Thank goodness she hadn't mentioned that. What if he'd turned her down flat? It would've hurt.

'See you.'

What was that about? Bella wondered as she climbed into her car. One minute all was good, then they start talking about when she was giving up work and his mood changed entirely. Whenever she chose to take leave was her business, not Aaron's, but lately she'd shared any information about her pregnancy plans with him. Too much? Was he getting cold feet? They were having a bit of a fling, nothing more. Definitely nothing serious enough to be making plans for a joint future. As much as she was falling for Aaron, she was not ready to step up and tell him so, nor was she ready to move in with him. Her baby had priority over every other decision she made in the coming months, and that meant not getting too involved with Aaron.

Her heart ached for what might've been if they'd met under normal circumstances. A fling possibly leading to a full-on relationship and then moving in together. That wasn't happening when she was pregnant with Jason's baby. Though to be fair, Aaron had never once hinted that he wouldn't care for a baby that wasn't his. She hadn't actually asked how he'd feel about that. It would sound as though she wanted to get involved full-time and they'd agreed that wasn't happening. Once Sophia arrived, she'd be too busy with her and work to continue the fling, let alone anything deeper and more fulfilling.

At home she headed for the shower and a long soak to ease the tension in her shoulders.

Men. Love them but they could tear you apart at times.

Bella sighed. No denying Aaron had got to her when she wasn't looking. She hadn't needed a man in her life, and still didn't. Except it wasn't so easy to believe that now she'd come to know this one, and let him into her heart when she wasn't thinking about it.

After drying herself, she wrapped the towel around her breasts and headed into the bedroom to find something to wear that was comfortable and yet didn't make her look dull and unattractive. If she did bump into Aaron at work she wanted him to take a second look.

A tune rang out on her phone.

Aaron.

'Hello.'

'Bella, I'm sorry for being obtuse. I get worried for you and it got out of hand this morning.'

The tension relaxed out of her body. 'Apology accepted.'

'Thank goodness. See you later?'

'Of course.' Then it dawned on her what might've put him in a funk this morning. 'Did you have a nightmare last night?' He hadn't had one during any of the few nights she'd stayed over but last night could've been the first.

'I did. I intended staying awake all night so I could keep an eye on you, but some time after two I must've dozed off.'

She hadn't been aware at all. 'You should've woken me. I could've hugged you until the gremlins went away.'

'You need your sleep at the moment.'

'Aaron,' she growled. 'We are there for each other. This is not a one-way relationship.'

Silence.

They hadn't called it a relationship before—because it was a fling, nothing more. Calling it a relationship meant getting deep and serious and, as she'd already had that discussion with herself this morning, she had nothing to say along those lines. 'What I meant—'

'I know where you're coming from, Bella. We're in this together and therefore we watch out for each other. My only issue is I'm not used to anyone doing that for me.'

Aaron handed his patient a prescription for analgesics. 'There you go. Take these until you run out. Don't stop when the pain decreases or you'll start using your arm and that wrist isn't ready to do any work.'

'*Grazie, Medico.* I will do as you say.'

The man's wife shook her head at him. 'Like you do me, huh?'

'Sì.'

Aaron smiled. These two hadn't stopped giving each other cheek since the man had presented querying a fractured wrist. Fortunately it was severely sprained, not broken, though a sprain could be as painful. 'Take care, and I hope I don't see you back here.'

'So do we,' the wife told him with a wide smile. 'Thank you for your help.' She took her husband's good arm and led him out of the department.

Aaron watched them go, wondering what it was like to be in such a loving relationship for so long. They'd know each other almost too well, but that had to be special. If only he got the opportunity to be a part of something similar.

Bella. It was annoying how her name kept banging around his head, along with an image of her beautiful face wearing a wide smile and cheerful eyes. Plus the one where she was fearful of something going wrong with her baby that made him want to reach out and hold her for ever and keep her safe.

She was in his heart now. No point denying it any longer even when he was trying his damnedest to remain careful. Hence his sudden abruptness with her that morning. Hearing her say she was going to work, and would continue doing so right till nearly the end of her pregnancy, had brought his protective instincts into play. Again he'd wanted to wrap her up and keep her safe.

He had no right to do so, or even to say anything about it, but it was hard not to when he cared about how this pregnancy went for her. She wanted her baby so much it was hurting her. To be nudged aside and basically told to mind his own business about what she chose to do in the coming months had hurt. It'd also been a timely reminder he didn't have any say in her decisions. The baby wasn't his. Though he'd love to be a surrogate dad for Sophia. As much as he'd love to pair up with Bella for the rest of their lives.

If only he could. But underneath these buoyant loving emotions he still feared being rejected once she came to fully understand her life would never be as private as it was now. She didn't put herself out there to be noticed, but there'd be no stopping the media once they learned she was in his life. He no longer even considered she might be interested in his family's fame and fortune. She wasn't rich, didn't have lots of high-end clothes and shoes, or live in a mansion, but didn't appear to want any of that either.

What she did have—and he didn't—was such a loving family that she was ensconced in happiness. In his book that came before all else. Jealous? Kind of. The real problem here was he was in too deep, couldn't pull out without hurting, and yet was afraid to risk taking a chance. Amy had hurt him so deeply, he knew when Bella realised she didn't want to put up with his lifestyle he'd be beyond hurt. Even if they stayed here, the media would follow them. It always did, no matter how hard he tried to get away.

'Aaron, a twenty-four-year-old man's being brought in by ambulance after a cycle accident on the hill. A metal object has penetrated his chest. His heart is erratic.'

'Bring him to the resus bed,' he told the junior doctor. All the equipment they'd need for X-rays, cardiac arrest, haemorrhaging and any other unforeseen event was on hand there. 'How far away is the ambulance?'

'Four minutes.'

'Right.' He went to scrub up. This sounded serious and the readier he was, the better.

CHAPTER EIGHT

BELLA STOOD UP and rubbed the small of her back. 'Luna, I'd better go over to the hospital and do a round before heading home.' Aaron might be somewhere in the building too. She had no real excuse to drop by the ED other than ask him to join the family for dinner. The thing was, she'd done that on Wednesday and he'd declined, said he had other things on. Like what? She hadn't asked, but felt peeved. He'd been as friendly as usual when she'd had to go into his department for a patient, but there'd been no phone conversations out of hours. So much for thinking everything was fine after his apology about being abrupt on Monday. Seemed he was still annoyed with her. She could try again, apologising and inviting him to dinner, but she wasn't going to. She didn't do kowtowing.

Nothing had changed when it came to how she felt about him. Her heart hadn't done a

U-turn, but whether it was good for her was something else to consider. Loving Aaron had come about so easily and naturally it was a little scary. When she fell for Jason it had been quick, and totally perfect, but there hadn't been a baby involved. A baby whose father was still a part of Bella's life and who she was, who she'd become.

Kick.

She laughed. Little Sophia had an innate sense of timing. 'Yes, little one, I'm thinking about your father.' What she was struggling with was how she'd love for her daughter to have a living father, a man who'd cherish her as much as Jason would've.

Kick.

Bella touched her stomach. 'What are you trying to tell me?'

Nothing.

'Great. So I have to make all the decisions?' Fair enough. Just not right now. Instead she'd go to the ED after she'd done a ward round and see if Aaron was still there. If so, she would invite him to join the family for dinner. It didn't mean she was planning a wedding or getting him to commit to anything. It was all about relaxing and being comfortable in each other's space. It didn't mean she expected to go back to his apartment afterwards to share his bed. She might want to, but only if he was in agreement, otherwise she'd feel awkward—and unwanted.

'I'm on duty till six so won't be able to make it till a bit later but if everyone's okay with that, I'd love to come,' Aaron told her when she found him filling in a patient's details in the ED and invited him to join her for dinner.

'No one clocks us in, so you'll be fine,' she said through a relieved smile.

A paramedic was pushing a patient into the department on a trolley. Aaron stood up. 'I'd better go.' But he didn't move away immediately. 'How have you been this week?'

Lonely. 'Good. No more twinges, just lots of kicks. I still think Sophia might be a footballer in waiting.'

His smile looked tired. Not sleeping well again?

'All those cousins will make sure of that.'

'I'd better go. See you later.'

'You will.'

She still felt he was uncomfortable joining

her but she wasn't going to push for reasons why. Could be he was stepping back to assess his feelings, as she'd done earlier. Better before baby arrived than afterwards when things could get complicated.

Baby Sophia. Everything came back to her and doing the right thing by her. To find her a father or to raise her alone with Jason in the background in the form of photos and words Bella could remember. She'd far prefer Sophia had a living, breathing *papà* who would read her bedtime stories and cuddle her, heat her milk and wipe away the tears, laugh at her antics and cry when she was sad. Jason would always be in the background. Always. But Sophia should have a *papà* at her side too.

Aaron was more than capable of being that man. He didn't turn away from responsibility or protecting those he cared about. His family weren't there for him in the way he'd like, but she doubted he'd ever walk away. As far as she could see that was Aaron, through and through. An ideal father figure.

An ideal partner for her? She wanted him to be, but wasn't certain. It was early days to even be wondering, but when she'd met Jason her attraction to him had happened in an instant. No doubts whatsoever. So to be having similar feelings for Aaron scared her into wanting to take time to get to know more about him in case she was trusting her instincts too much just because they'd worked well the first time.

'Thought you were heading home.' The man confusing her usually clear thinking appeared before her. 'You are all right, Bella?'

'Yes, I'm fine. I was just thinking about… About—a patient.'

Pathetic. No patient would want anything to do with her if that was all she could come up with when Aaron queried her state of health. But she was hardly going to admit her mind had been on him. Not when he'd been wary around her lately.

'Save it for Monday. Go home and take a break before dinner.'

He could be quite bossy without any real effort, she realised as she tramped along the corridor to the back exit. Used to getting his own way? If he was, he didn't overdo it. Or hadn't with her. Something to watch out for? Or she could ignore it and go with the flow, learn more about him without looking for pointers that might lead her in the wrong direction, which sounded far easier than the first option.

Shoving Aaron out of her head on the short drive home, she thought about her wardrobe and what to wear tonight. Not a lot of choice unless she was okay with looking like a beached whale. It seemed only days ago she could slip into any of the dresses or trousers hanging in her wardrobe and feel comfortable in a fashionable, and a little bit sexy, way. Not any more.

Bring on the shopping expedition she planned doing while visiting Jason's parents at the weekend. Nothing better to make her feel good about herself than some new outfits that highlighted her good features and dulled the not so good. Baby certainly had altered her shape dramatically in a hurry. While she was excited about that, she still wanted to look good—hot—so Aaron couldn't ignore her.

Pathetic. If he wasn't interested, why bother? She didn't want to drag a man into her arms, preferred he come flying at her because he couldn't resist her. Their fling had to mean he did find her attractive. Didn't it? 'So, what to wear tonight? For an everyday meal with the family who'd not notice anyway? OTT, Bella girl.' Yeah, well, sometimes that was her. Especially with Aaron in the picture.

She chose sky-blue three-quarter trousers and a chintzy white blouse that dipped to her growing cleavage and showed off her tanned skin to perfection. Staring at her image in the mirror, twisting this way and that, she had to admit her breasts were filling out quite nicely. Give them another month or two and they'd probably be ginormous and she'd be hating them, but for now she could be happy with how they filled out the front of the blouse to perfection. There were some pluses to growing a belly so fast it looked like a balloon that someone had forgotten to stop pumping full of oxygen.

Aaron crossed the restaurant to the seat next to Bella, his eyes entirely focused on the beautiful sight before him. She got more attractive by the day, and she'd started out close to perfect in the first place. How was he going to walk away at the end of his contract? It was all very well saying he was protecting his heart, but he was already too late for that. So he'd stick to the fact that he would do anything to keep Bella safe from the media hype. So why had he agreed to come here tonight? Because he just couldn't turn her down. Couldn't not be with her.

'Evening, Bella.' Leaning in, he placed a light kiss on her cheek. Light. Not sexy or deep. Damn it.

Deep green eyes met his gaze. 'Hi. You got away on time, then?'

'Despite what you said, I couldn't risk Gino refusing to feed me because I was late.'

From the far end of the table, Gino laughed. 'So I scare you more than a patient? Perfect.' He might be joking, but Aaron was aware that the moment he did something to hurt Bella, Gino would be on his case in an instant. Which only backed up his own thoughts about staying away from getting too close. Hard, if not impossible, to give up a fling that was making him happy in so many ways he once hadn't believed possible though.

'Ignore him,' Bella whispered close to him.

Breathing in roses, he leaned back in his chair and laughed. 'That's like suggesting I wear a jersey to dinner. Impossible.' The outside temperature had been posted at twenty-eight last time he'd looked, an hour ago. Inside the restaurant the air-conditioning was doing its bit to keep it down but there was no avoiding the fact it was a hot day. The heat had slapped him in the face when he'd walked out of ED at the end of his shift and he was still reeling. Edinburgh didn't quite match Stresa when it came to summer temperatures.

'I'm hoping for slightly cooler in London. Though the shops are usually cool enough to enjoy. I think the owners know having good air-conditioning keeps customers happy and in the shop, and therefore buying their goods.'

'What time are you flying out?'

'I catch the nine o'clock flight.' Which meant an early train to Milan.

'Want me to drive you to the airport?' he offered.

'Thanks, but I've got it sorted. What have you planned for the weekend?' she asked.

'I haven't been to Como so figured tomorrow is as good a day as any. I'll take my walking shoes and find a track to hike.' The more walking he did, the more he wanted to do. It was turning out to be so good for his stress levels.

He thought about the attack often as he strode along and for some inexplicable reason the fear didn't raise its head. Now that only happened in the dark of night, and not when Bella was with him, except they hadn't got together in his bed this week.

If only he'd leapt out of bed and headed away at the crack of dawn on Saturday morning, Aaron reflected through a moment of despair when he opened his door on hearing the chime ring to find his sister standing on the doorstep with a suitcase.

'Surprise,' cried Maggie as she wrapped him in a hug.

'You could say that,' he muttered as he hugged her back.

'I got tired of waiting for you to come home to see me before I head away so I decided to drop in and hassle you.' Maggie laughed. 'You'd better not say you're working this weekend because I already checked.'

'You did?' Someone had told his sister he wasn't rostered on?

'A nurse who was more than happy to talk

about you said you had the whole weekend off so no excuses for not spending time with me.'

'Sounds good.' He meant it. They mightn't be the closest family about, but he loved his sister and spending time with her was great. He automatically glanced down the path to the road. No cameras, no nosey reporters to spoil the moment. Yet. Thank goodness Bella was out of town for the weekend. 'Come in and get a load off.'

'Not bad,' his sister said as she looked around the house. 'Stunning view, though awfully quiet.'

'That's one of the reasons I like living here.'

'How long have you got left on your contract?'

'A couple of months.' Maybe a lot more if he got around to making up his mind about his future and Bella. 'After that, who knows?'

'You're not thinking of walking away from your position in Edinburgh?'

Sometimes Maggie read him too easily. Like Bella. 'Nothing's definite. Stresa's wonderful and there must be other towns around Italy where I could work.'

'Me thinks there's someone here keeping you

entertained.' Maggie picked up an obviously female sweater. 'A woman who might be pressing some buttons, huh?'

From a sweater to a relationship? Only Maggie would come up with that. True as it was, he wasn't talking about Bella. Maggie would never stop asking more questions he had no firm answers for, so he downplayed the question. 'No harm in a little activity outside work.'

'No harm in finding the right one, either.'

'I was about to make breakfast when you turned up. Have you eaten?'

'Coffee and a stale bun on the train doesn't count.'

'Then I'll whip up something while you put the coffee on.'

'Let's go out. I want to see the town and get the feel of the place you think so highly of.'

Aaron shivered. Go out, and have Maggie recognised? In Stresa? Not likely, unless an overzealous reporter had followed her here, which happened often enough to make him edgy. 'You sure you're on your own?'

'I overnighted in Milan and if anyone was going to make themselves known that's when

I'd have noticed.' She wouldn't have been looking very hard.

'There's a patisserie a few kilometres away towards the town centre. We'll go there.'

'Whatever.' Maggie shrugged. 'You know the area.'

Yes, and which restaurant to avoid while you're in town.

Maggie was not going near Gino's.

'I've named her already,' Bella told Jason's parents as they gazed at the scan image she'd given them.

She'd spent the afternoon wandering through the local market with Jason's mother, and checking out a few shops, trying to get comfortable with her. Normally it wasn't so hard, but the thought of how close she was getting to Aaron kept her wondering how these two would accept him if he became a serious part of her life.

'What have you chosen?' Justine Wright asked.

'Sophia Justine.'

Justine gasped. 'You've used my name for her middle one?' A small smile followed the question. 'Thank you, Bella.'

'It's a no-brainer. Sophia was my grandmother's name.' Jason's parents had been disappointed she'd never taken their surname when they married but for her it had been a show of independence. Not every woman took her husband's name these days and Rosso was on all her medical certificates, something she was proud of. She was a Rosso through and through. It seemed she'd made Justine happy about this though.

'It brings Jason a bit closer,' Colin admitted as he continued to stare at the framed image.

'He is Sophia's father, and I will make sure she knows about him. You being in her life will strengthen whatever I tell her. I'm never going to keep her from seeing you.' Bella had lost count of the number of times she'd told them, but it seemed they couldn't quite accept it.

'What happens if you meet another man, remarry?' Justine asked.

Bella felt her face warm. 'Nothing changes in that Jason is still Sophia's father. Naturally if I do find another partner he will be a big part of her life, or I wouldn't want him.'

Colin was watching her closely. 'Have you met someone?'

Here we go.

Best to be upfront though she knew it was going to hurt these two. The truth was it would hurt them ten years from now. Jason had been their only child and they were struggling to move on. 'I've been dating a doctor who's working in Stresa temporarily. So far it's nothing serious.' Pants on fire? 'I'm very hesitant about getting close to someone after Jason. We had a wonderful marriage, and, honestly, my main focus is my pregnancy and the baby.'

'You have to be open to another relationship, Bella,' Colin said, surprising the air out of her lungs. Never would she have expected him to say that. He'd always been so closed when it came to her moving on from Jason's death. 'All we ask is that you be careful, take your time.'

Sounded to Bella as if Colin and Justine had discussed this. 'Thank you. I'll always be open with you both. You're part of my life, and that's not going to change no matter what lies ahead.'

Justine surprised her further by standing up and crossing over to give her a rare hug, which told her how much they cared for her. 'Thanks,' she whispered. 'None of this is easy but you've just made it a little more so.'

'Right.' Justine stepped away and brushed her hands down the front of her trousers. 'You said you intend to go shopping tomorrow before flying out. How about we go into the city together and have some fun? I'd love to buy some clothes for Sophia and you can make sure you like my choices.'

Another surprise. Not a person to enjoy shopping with others because it always took twice as long, nonetheless she couldn't say no. That'd undo all the ground she'd made up today.

'Sounds perfect. I need to find some outfits that will see me through the coming months.' She gave a little grin. 'I can't wait to see what's available for my baby girl either.' Then she rubbed the small of her back. 'I'm going to bed now if you don't mind. I seem to get tired all too easily these days.' It was barely nine o'clock but all she wanted to do was lie down somewhere quiet. Thinking about Aaron and how he'd fit in and how Jason's parents might react had drained her. The fact they'd said she had to be open about another relationship was good but added to the pressure somehow. She'd have to get it right or they'd never forgive her. It was also strange how little she was thinking about Jason when she was here. Seemed she was looking forward more and less at the past.

'See you in the morning, Bella.'

As she lay between the crisp white sheets, Aaron slid into her head yet again. What was he doing? Dinner with Tommaso maybe. They got on well and had taken to visiting the inn together one night a week. She suspected Tommaso was partly getting onside with Aaron to help entice him to stay on at the end of his contract as it wasn't easy finding specialists for the small hospital. Chances were Aaron wouldn't stay. He had pointed out he still had a job to return to in Scotland, and he probably preferred the more intense departments of larger hospitals. She hoped he might change his mind—if that meant he wanted more with her, that was.

Loving Aaron had come about so easily and naturally it was a bit scary. It was different from when she fell for Jason. That had been quick too, and totally perfect. But there hadn't been a baby involved. A baby whose father was still a large part of who she was, who she'd become.

Kick.

Warmth filled her. 'Yes, little one, I'm thinking about you and your *papà*.' But she'd love her daughter to have a living father, a man who'd cherish her as much as Jason would've if he'd been here. Aaron was caring and compassionate, and loving. Yes, she could see him in the role of Sophia's *papà*. Jason might even have agreed.

Kick.

Bella touched her stomach. 'What are you trying to tell me?'

Kick.

'You're persistent, aren't you?' Picking up the novel she'd brought with her, she tried to divert her mind by reading, except the words blurred as her head filled with Aaron. She needed to learn more about him and his reticence was starting to rub her up the wrong way. She'd been open about her love for Jason and her future and her family and anything he wanted to know. Come to think of it, he didn't ask a lot of questions about her. That might be because he didn't want to reciprocate.

His mother was an actress, his sister a camera operator making a name for herself, his father a high court judge.

Sighing with frustration, she reached for her

tablet. It wasn't the way to find out about Aaron's family but neither could she wait for him to decide when it was time to talk about them.

As she didn't know anyone's first name she keyed in Aaron Marshall and held her breath while waiting for the screen to deliver.

Aaron Marshall wasn't an uncommon name, but only one on the screen was an emergency specialist practising in Edinburgh. Slightly out of date, but the photo of Aaron dressed in hospital scrubs looking anything but pleased to be in the limelight snagged her attention. He was so gorgeous. Sexy as, and so good-looking her mouth watered. The headline read: *Judge Marshall's son attacked by knife-wielding man in ED.*

Numerous entries followed, all with Aaron's name in the headline. Aaron in a tux, dressed in hiking trousers and shirt with a pack on his back, wearing a suit heading into a theatre where his mother was performing. In each and every one of the photos he looked confident and unassailable. Every photo made her heart squeeze a little harder.

She adored him.

She stared at the screen. Putting up with the

media at every turn must be hell. Delving further, Bella found Maggie Marshall, the camera operator who'd won awards for her work with a movie camera, Diane Marshall the actress in a current British television saga, and the judge, John Marshall, who'd sentenced a local parliamentarian to six years for embezzlement that the man still swore he hadn't had anything to do with.

Shutting down the website, Bella slid the tablet onto the bedside table and snuggled down under the covers. There was a lot more to Aaron than she'd supposed despite what he'd told her about his family getting quite a lot of attention. He'd held back on the details. Not that she could blame him. It showed he wasn't into all the hurrah. He'd said as much, but she hadn't realised how well known his family was. No wonder Stresa was a calm place for him. Could that play a part in his decision to move to Italy?

Thump, thump, went her heart. Was she reading too much into this because she'd love him to move to her home town permanently?

Looked as if the time had arrived for them to have a serious discussion about their relationship. No more messing around. Either they were together or they weren't.

Spending time with Jason's parents had made her realise she was ready to move forward and have a complete future.

She was ready to accept him into her life, and into Sophia's life.

Yes, she definitely was. This had nothing to do with his family and who they were, but the fact he didn't flaunt it, and, she suspected, rued it a lot of the time, made her love him even more. She was ready.

CHAPTER NINE

THE PLATFORM WAS crowded as Bella stepped off the train at Stresa, hauling her now overfull case behind her. 'Wonder what's going on?' she said to the woman she'd been sitting beside on the trip from Milano, a friend from school days.

'I'd say everyone's waiting for the southbound train,' Terese said as she looked around. 'I'm glad we weren't affected as I'm on duty in two hours.'

Bella stifled a yawn, grateful not to be working until tomorrow. 'You weren't leaving any room for error, then.'

Terese laughed. 'Hugo said he'd cover for me if I was late.'

'You got a good one there.'

'I know.' The love in her voice spoke volumes, and had Bella remembering when it had been like that for her and Jason.

It also got her wondering if she could have

it again with Aaron. Whenever she thought of him that wonderful warm, soft feeling of wonder filled her head and heart and had her daydreaming of wonderful things. Shaking her head to clear away those thoughts, she pushed through the crowd. 'Let's get out of here.'

'Maggie, there's nothing you can do about this but be patient.'

The voice that filled her dreams last night had her turning around to scan the sea of heads. 'Aaron? Is that you?'

'Bella? Hey there. I wasn't expecting to bump into you, but then I didn't think my sister's train would be running so late. It was held up by a truck hitting a car on a crossing further north but now it's only minutes away.'

His sister was here? He hadn't mentioned anything about her visiting over the weekend. Bella shrugged. He didn't have to let her know everything that was going on in his life, but she couldn't help feeling left out of something. They were better than that, surely? 'Catch up later. I'm getting out of here.'

'Hey, wait.' His hand was on her arm. 'You'd better meet Maggie.' He was making an effort, if a little late.

'Sure, but can we move away from the crowd? I'm getting a lot of elbows in my side and stomach.'

Annoyance crossed his face. For her being knocked about or because she wanted to be somewhere quieter, she didn't know, but she wasn't standing here any longer. 'I'm going downstairs to the entrance.'

'Maggie, follow me. I want you to meet someone.' Aaron still held her arm and now he was reaching for her case with his other hand. 'Give me that.'

She wasn't incapable, but it was nice having a man taking care of her. 'Sure. Watch out. It's heavy.' She'd done a fair amount of shopping for herself and Sophia. Then there were the toys and tiny dresses and outfits Justine had bought adding to the weight. Thank goodness for expandable cases with wheels.

At the bottom of the stairs Aaron led her to a corner away from the frustrated crowd milling about.

She'd have preferred to go outside but realised that his sister would want to get on the train as soon as it arrived so even coming down the stairway was a bonus. When she looked at

Aaron, her chest tightened. She'd missed him more than she'd have believed. 'Your plans for the weekend changed?'

'Maggie turned up unannounced yesterday morning.'

'Since Aaron was being tardy about coming to London to catch up before I head across to the USA I decided to gatecrash his weekend.' A stunning woman of a similar age to Bella stood before her. 'I'm Maggie, Aaron's annoying sister. You must be Bella.'

'That's me.' So Aaron had mentioned her. Or had Maggie heard him call out to her on the platform? 'I hear you're moving to America?'

'In four weeks, and with the weeks flying past and getting busier by the day, I grabbed the opportunity to come across to catch up with Aaron while it was still possible. There's so much to do with the current programme I'm working on while getting up to speed with the film I'm going to be involved with in LA.' The woman could talk, for sure.

A light flashed behind them.

Aaron's mouth tightened.

Maggie didn't blink.

Bella glanced around, wondering what was

going on, and saw a man holding a large camera above the people standing in groups as they waited for the next train. The camera was pointed in their direction. She already had her back to him so she turned her head back to face Maggie and Aaron. 'It's great you could make it over here. Did Aaron show you the sights or were you both too busy talking to go anywhere?'

'The sights and the eateries. We took the cable car up the hill and the views are stupendous. No wonder he likes Stresa so much. It might be hard to get him to return to Edinburgh.'

That's what I'm hoping, Bella admitted to herself.

'Too quiet for me,' Maggie carried on. 'I love big, busy, noisy cities.'

'We didn't go to Gino's,' Aaron said sharply. 'Though Maggie wanted to. I wasn't having her followers tagging along and upsetting things in the restaurant. Gino would've kicked my backside.'

Gino would've made the most of it and suggested the reporters take a table and order a meal like none they'd had before. He'd also have made sure no one left their table to harass any other diners, including her family. 'I expect the restaurant was busy.' The tourist season was in full swing so Gino's was buzzing every night, though her brother would've made sure Aaron got a table.

'I understand you're a paediatrician,' Maggie was saying, her eyes giving Bella the once-over at the same time. 'A pregnant one, at that.'

So? 'Yes, I am both of those.' The words came out a little sharper than she'd intended but she didn't like the way Maggie was eyeing her up.

'Take no notice of me. I often speak before thinking. I didn't mean to insult you. Nor upset you. Having a baby must be exciting.'

'It is.'

The loudspeaker interrupted all talk. 'Passengers travelling to Milan are to go to platform two as your train will arrive in two minutes.'

Maggie threw her arms around her brother. 'See you in LA, Aaron. Bring Bella with you. I want to get to know her better.'

'We'll see,' Aaron growled before returning the hug. 'Take care and make a success of the movie.'

'Why wouldn't I?' Maggie grinned, then turned to Bella. 'I mean it. Come and visit when Aaron does. Bring baby with you.'

This woman was full on, but underneath all the talk Bella suspected she might be a bit lonely. 'As Aaron said, let's wait and see. All the best with your movie.'

'Thanks.' Maggie was already turning to rush up the stairs. 'Guess I'll have to fight my way to a seat.'

'Come on. Let's get out of here while everyone's focused on reaching the platform.' Again Aaron had her arm in one hand and case in the other. 'With a bit of luck the reporters following Maggie will bc on the train with her.'

'Why wouldn't they?' she asked when they reached the outside.

'Because they are unpredictable, and if they sense a story elsewhere they'll hang around like a dog sniffing a bone.'

'So you're a bone?' She laughed.

His face was grim as he shook his head. 'You don't understand. Until now the media didn't know where I was working, and probably didn't care too much as I haven't done anything worthy of reporting lately. Unfortunately now they've seen me with you there are bound to be questions about our relationship.'

'What relationship?' The question was out before she knew she was going to ask it.

'Not the one we know we have, but whatever they choose to make up for a good headline. I shouldn't have called out to you when I saw you in the crowd. It was instinctive. I'd missed you and there you were looking happy and beautiful and I just couldn't wait to be with you.'

'Aaron, it's all good. No one's going to take the slightest bit of notice of me. Why would they? I'm a local doctor, nothing more.'

Flash. Another camera appeared in front of them.

'Bugger off,' Aaron said under his breath.

But she'd heard and felt the tension increasing in his grip on her arm.

Flash.

'This is exactly what I was warning you about.'

'Aaron, tell us about your partner. Who is she? When's the baby due? How do you feel about becoming a father?'

Bella's head whipped up and she stared at the

man standing directly in front of them. 'Excuse me. You're in my way.'

'What's your name, lady? Are you from around here?'

'If you don't mind getting out of my way. I am not talking to you.'

'How long have you known Aaron Marshall?'

Bella ignored him and walked straight at him so he had to step aside or look stupid when she bumped into him.

'You're carrying his baby.'

Bile soured her mouth. What right did this man have to pluck ideas out of the air and put them on her? She continued walking, head high, mouth tight.

Aaron's hand was steady around hers as he said, 'Fergusson, you couldn't be further from the truth if you tried so how about leaving us alone? We'd appreciate it.' Then he added quiet enough for only her to hear, 'Like that's going to happen. I am sorry, Bella.'

She refused to look anywhere but in the direction she was headed. This wasn't an entirely new experience. 'Not your fault,' she said just as quietly.

'Lady, when's your baby due?'

Bella stopped, drew a breath and locked her eyes on the despicable man. 'That's none of your business, as are none of the answers to the other questions you asked. I will not be talking to you about anything.' She started walking again, head high, heart thumping and her hand tight in Aaron's.

'You're no wimp,' Aaron muttered. 'But I have to warn you, it won't work. Not unless there's a bomb blast in the next few minutes. My car's over there.'

Relief at being able to shortly shut the door on the reporter filled her. 'That's better than walking down the hill to home.' It was barely a kilometre to the apartment but that was a long way if she was going to be plagued by nosey reporters who had nothing better to do with their time. It was none of their business who her baby's father was, or that she was pregnant, or that she and Aaron were close. Pressing her lips tight, she headed to Aaron's car and tugged the door open the moment he flicked the locking device.

'So much for getting home and having time to unpack and get ready for the coming week after a lovely weekend in London.'

'You enjoyed your time with Jason's parents?' Aaron was pulling out of the car park before he'd even closed his door.

'Did I say that out loud? Yes, it was good.' Only she'd been brought back to reality in a hurry. A new reality. She was beginning to seethe at the rude behaviour of that reporter. Her life had nothing to do with him and would be as dull as dishwater to anyone reading whatever story he could come up with. 'Who does he think he is?'

'Someone who believes he has the right to ask personal questions and then share the answers with readers.' Aaron had got who she was talking about. 'Not all reporters are like him, only the worst, but Maggie and my family seem to attract those ones along with the respectful ones.'

'It wasn't Maggie he was harassing.'

'He had been. Which makes it even more stupid of me for coming over to you.'

'You can't live your life dodging what you want because of people like him.' Whenever Jason had made the headlines she'd tended to keep out of the picture, but she hadn't stopped doing the things she'd wanted to.

'Believe me, I've made it an art form.'

'So they win.' Of course, she hadn't been exposed to anything like what she was starting to realise Aaron had. She might've reacted differently when with Jason if the intensity and regularity of reporters and their questions had been more aggressive and frequent.

'Not always.' Aaron pulled up outside the restaurant, which thankfully hadn't opened yet. 'I won't come in.'

So much for catch-up time. If she weren't so angry at the reporter she'd have laughed at herself. Catch up after a couple of days apart? But she'd missed Aaron, even when she was busy shopping or having dinner with her in-laws. Her anger increased. 'So he wins,' she repeated scathingly.

'I can't—no, I won't cause more problems for you, or any for Gino and his restaurant for that matter.'

'Gino can handle things.'

'You have no idea how persistent that man can be, or what he'll do to get inside info on you and your family.'

'How do you know that? You don't know the half of what my family have done over the years.' Now her anger was focused on Aaron. All she wanted was to be with him and here he was, doing his utmost to get away from her.

'Bella, believe me when I say I've seen the worst of him, and others like him. There's no dealing with them. Now that Fergusson has seen me holding hands with a pregnant woman he's not going to go away quietly. I'm trying to protect you.' He didn't reach for her hands as he usually did when he was being serious. There wasn't a hint of longing in his face; more like a look of withdrawal.

She stared at him, her anger boiling over. 'Are you sure it's just me you're protecting?'

His mouth opened, closed again. Then he shoved his door open and removed her case from the back seat and wheeled it to the building's entrance.

She followed, her anger dissipating in an instant as she waited for him to turn around and haul her into his arms and kiss away this nightmare. To tell her he was wrong, they were a couple and would get through whatever happened as a team.

'I'm sorry it's come to this, Bella.' He strode past her, back to his car. Then he drove away.

Not a word. No answer to her question. Nothing. *Niente.* A very cold shoulder from the man who'd been so caring. If he couldn't talk then there was no hope for them. Talking was important.

Her heart cracked as his car disappeared around the corner. There was a lot he didn't know about her. It included the fact she loved him. Because she hadn't told him. She wasn't any better at talking. She didn't want to risk her heart a second time. Losing her first love had been hard, and she couldn't face that again.

Except she already had.

CHAPTER TEN

AARON CHECKED HIS rear-view mirror as he turned into his drive. Still no one following, but then there hadn't been time for Fergusson to get a car before he'd driven Bella away from the station. He liked to be prepared, not blindsided with a camera in his face. Fingers crossed the man had boarded the train to stay near to Maggie and note what she was up to.

Maybe, but unlikely if the guy already knew Maggie was returning to London. He wanted to get mad at his sister for visiting, but he couldn't. They were close in their own way, and he'd been happy to see her. But to have Bella accosted like that and asked about the baby and the father made his blood boil. He should never have got so close to her, should never have fallen for her.

But I have.

There lay the problem. He had to walk away, leave Bella to get on with her life and have her baby and raise her in the best way possible—without photographers and infuriating reporters hanging around every corner. Leaving her meant hurting himself, but he was doing it because he loved her. Yeah, sure.

'Are you sure it's just me you're protecting?' Bella's question echoed in his head. He'd known she was no slug when it came to understanding him, but he hadn't expected that. Because truthfully? He was looking out for himself. He didn't want to end up heartbroken again. Only problem was—it was already too late. He was hurting big time.

What happened next? He'd love to see her and have a deep and meaningful talk. The only problem with that was at the end they'd still go their separate ways, especially once Bella understood how harrowing all the publicity could be.

To hell with this. He needed air and space and time to think without anyone interrupting. Not that there was anyone in his apartment, but he could picture Bella sitting on his deck or on the couch or lying in his bed curled into him, or making love.

Grabbing his hiking boots, Aaron headed

out of the door. Away from searing memories, away from confronting the fact he'd well and truly messed up, and on with his future. Without Bella Rosso in it.

His phone pinged.

Bella.

Ignoring her wasn't the answer. He had to tell her in no uncertain terms they were no longer an item. Their fling was over. 'Hello.'

'Can you come over to my apartment, please? We can't turn our backs on what we have. Not without talking about it first anyway.' She wasn't pleading, or sounding as if he'd pulled the floor out from underneath her. More as though she was being strong and coping better than he was, which suggested she wasn't as involved as he was.

She had said they couldn't ignore what they had between them. He had to. For her sake as well as his. 'There's nothing more to say, Bella. I'm sorry it ended this way, but I don't want to continue with our fling any longer. There was always an end date approaching. It's arrived sooner than expected but nevertheless it's here.'

'You don't want a full-on relationship, then?

One where we help each other through the awful times and love the good ones?'

'No, I don't.'

I can't. Someone has to look out for my heart and that comes down to me.

'I never did, and I don't think I ever indicated otherwise.'

That was met with silence. Who knew silence could be so loud? It was as though the air were thick with hurt and anger and disappointment.

And guilt. Oh, yes. Guilt filled him, twisted his gut, clouded his head and brought tears to his eyes. Guilt for hurting her. For upsetting her. For letting her down—though that was a two-way issue because this was all about protecting her—*and* himself.

'I can't argue with that.' Bella cut through his turbulent thoughts. 'But I thought you were getting more into us than what you're showing now. Guess I read you wrong.' She paused.

He waited, the breath stuck in the back of his throat.

'Or not.' *Click.* She was gone.

Leaving Aaron confused. No, not confused, but rattled, because once again Bella was showing him how well she had come to understand him. If only he could go around to her apartment and take her in his arms and hold on for ever. But he'd done that with Amy when she'd said she couldn't cope and she'd pushed him aside, said she didn't love him enough to live with his family's noise. This time it was him not coping and so pushing Bella away.

Noise. That was Amy's word for all the turbulence. He actually got it. It was noise. Loud and intrusive at its best. While Bella seemed to want to pursue what they'd started he understood the slow eating-away at a person's resilience the noise did and therefore how the day would still come when she'd pack her bags for good.

Yes, he loved her and was hurting, but to become a true couple in the eyes of her family, and then watch her walk away, would be excruciating. Maybe he was a coward. He did want love and family. More than anything else. Almost.

How was he going to manage avoiding her when they had to work together at times? So much for considering applying for the permanent position in the department. He'd always known the day would come when he'd have to accept he couldn't stay and fit in with Bella and her daughter. Of course he'd known and had done from the first time he'd sat down at the Rosso family dinner table beside Bella and relaxed in a way he hadn't ever truly done before.

Then go see her, have that talk she wanted, explain yourself.

He kept striding along the pathway, heading out of town, away from the tourists and locals and Bella.

'This is Katie White,' Aaron told Bella when she stepped into the cubicle a nurse had indicated. 'She's got a temperature of thirty-nine and complains of sharp aches in both ears.'

'Hello, Katie. I'm Bella Rosso, a doctor, and I'm going to see what's going on with you.' Bella turned to the woman sitting by the bed. 'You're Katie's mother?'

'Yes. Katie's never had anything like this before.'

'Dr Marshall says you have an infection in both ears, Katie. We need to find out what's causing them.'

Dr Marshall was still in the cubicle. Never

had she called Aaron 'Dr' when with a patient, but they'd become somewhat remote with each other in the hospital over the last five days. It had to stop. They were being ridiculous, childish even.

'Katie doesn't seem to have any other infected areas and her ears have been painful for more than two days,' Aaron said.

Bella continued. 'We'll take swabs and send them to the lab, but they take a couple of days for the results to come back. In the meantime we'll put you on antibiotics. First I want to take a look at your ears and listen to your breathing and heart.'

After examining Katie and organising laboratory tests, Bella headed back to the ward to check on little Francesco, who was recovering from a severe bout of asthma. She hated walking away from Aaron but confronting him at work wasn't professional. Besides, he seemed determined to keep the barriers up, only talking about patients whenever she was called to the ED. It was as though they'd never slept together, or gone for a walk, or laughed and talked. When she had tried to mention anything that didn't involve work he'd clammed up, or been particularly polite and walked away. No wonder she wasn't sleeping or even eating proper meals. She was hurting, badly.

After looking in on Francesco, she spent time on the computer updating files and checking other patient results from the lab and Radiology, before deciding it was time to go home to her quiet, empty apartment.

Out at her car she hesitated, tempted to go and find Aaron and ask him to call in on his way home so they could at least talk, but, looking around the car park, she couldn't see his car so he must've already finished for the day.

She'd see if he was at home. He wasn't. Calling his phone got her nowhere either, other than to leave a message. 'Aaron, give me a call when you're free.'

He must've had a very busy night because he didn't ring.

When Bella was called into the emergency department two days later he was nowhere to be seen. 'Aaron not on shift?' she asked Tommaso.

'He swapped with me so I can go to my son's tennis game tonight. I was surprised really as he doesn't like night shifts.'

He was avoiding her. He won. She'd stop trying to make contact. She got the message. Aaron did not want anything more to do with her.

Then late Friday afternoon he called her to see a two-year-old girl. 'Greta has epilepsy but I would like you to check her before we allow her to go home with her mother.'

Nothing unusual in that. 'On my way.'

When she walked into the department Aaron stood up from his desk and crossed to join her, unlike other days this week. 'Thanks for this. I'm sure Greta's fine but her *mamma* is overwrought with worry so I thought you might be able to calm her down.' There was even a small smile on that divine mouth.

For her? A quick look around told her no one else was near. 'Let's get this sorted.' Did a softening in his stance mean he was starting to see things differently? She wasn't pushing for more. He'd probably close down on her again.

Twenty minutes later she stood up from the computer and picked up her bag. Work was over for the week, and she was so tired. Her whole body ached with weariness. Not so much because work had been busy but because sleep had been as elusive as snow in summer. She missed Aaron. Seeing him in here on the occasions she'd been called to the department didn't make up for sharing a meal or a hug or making love. Especially since he seemed determined to stay uninvolved. Too late. She couldn't be much more involved if she tried. 'Goodnight, Aaron.'

'Have a good weekend, Bella.'

That was likely the last thing she'd have, wondering where he was and what he was doing. Though he was definitely warming a little. 'Would you like to join me for dinner tonight?' she asked thoughtlessly.

'I don't think so. Thanks anyway.'

She couldn't help the next things to come out of her mouth. 'I can't believe how you've cut me off so completely. What's wrong with sharing a meal with me?' It was almost as if she didn't exist and they hadn't had a fling and talked about their futures.

'Fergusson's back in town. He tried to talk to me this morning.' Aaron leaned against the doorframe. 'Since he put that photo of you and I online along with the article about Maggie you are fair game for any reporter to do a number on you. Especially if I'm anywhere near you.'

The article hadn't pleased her but she'd shrugged it away. Nothing she could do to make it disappear. The postulating about her baby's father made her teeth grind, as did the guessing going on about the relationship Aaron was having with her, but she'd ride it out. Her life was boring by most people's standards and eventually she'd be yesterday's news. 'I've been here before and survived. I'll manage this time.' So much for thinking he was softening. She headed down the corridor.

'What do you mean? This isn't new to you?' Aaron was keeping pace with her, which in itself was new for this week.

'I told you Jason occasionally hit the headlines with something he'd done in his medical field which saved a patient who'd had no chance. When that happened I'd be pursued for a bit of scandal about the medical specialist's life.' It had been vile the way those scumbag reporters had thought they could do that, but she'd stayed cool and eventually they'd got fed up with her and gone to find someone far more intriguing.

'I didn't think it through.'

'Maybe I should've explained more but it had nothing to do with our relationship and therefore I didn't bother.' Why would she when she'd worked hard to avoid talking about that time in their lives where she and Jason didn't always see eye to eye about what was going on? He'd loved the limelight. She'd hated it. Still did, but that didn't mean she was going to run and hide if confronted again. She had a life to live and she wasn't stopping. Her chin dropped. With or without Aaron.

He was still with her. Interesting. 'Fair enough. I didn't come forward about my family in the beginning, and certainly never mentioned how intense the media got when it came to my mother and sister.' That was more than he'd said to her all week unless talking about patients.

Bella kept walking, not wanting to give him cause to head away in another direction. 'For you, it's important, I know. You want me to understand and be prepared.' So why hadn't he explained earlier?

'I do.' Aaron sighed. 'I admit to enjoying the weeks I had when no one knew who I was and anything about my background. I didn't want it to stop. I believed you'd never abuse it, but there've been some tough lessons in my past when it comes to trusting women and how they react to the fuss that goes on at times, and I can't forget them.'

Now she had to look at him. Her heart felt heavy for what he might've missed out on in the past. No matter they weren't seeing eye to eye or that he'd snubbed her all week, her heart skipped as she drank in that sexy face.

'Aaron, I can't say I understand everything but you have to be loyal to yourself first and foremost. Protecting your heart is a part of that, but please don't think we're all the same. I am not interested in the nonsense that obviously goes on in the background of your life, but that doesn't mean I want to walk away from you. Not without knowing we can't make a go of what we started anyway.'

'Ah, Bella. If only it was that simple.'

'Why can't it be?'

'I don't think I'm ready.'

Of course she overcomplicated things when it came to her love for Aaron. She was always looking for what could go wrong and not what was so good about being with him, yet now she was ready to take the last step to be by his side for ever.

'Will you ever be?'

The entrance door slid open. 'Bella, Aaron, look this way. We want a photo of the both of you together.' Fergusson was back.

'Not now.' Bella drew a breath, held her head high, and continued on out to the car park and her car. By now the reporters knew where she worked and lived, what she drove, probably what she ate so she wasn't bothering with trying to hide in plain sight. If only everything else were that straightforward.

Aaron watched the love of his life walk out of the building as if there were nothing unusual going on. Dignified came to mind. Bella had an air about her that said, 'Don't mess with me.' Not that Fergusson and his ilk took a lot of notice, but neither did they get right into her space as they were prone to do with others.

'Leave her be, Fergusson. Miss Rosso has nothing to say that'll make you top reporter for the week.' Aaron followed Bella to her car and opened the door for her to get in. 'Take care,' he said quietly.

'No other way to go,' she said as she touched the ignition button.

Aaron looked at her hard. Tears were slipping from the corners of her eyes. 'Bella?'

'See you around.' She grabbed the door and pulled it shut with a bang.

She was losing it. Big time. Bella didn't do tears. Not that he'd seen anyway. Was this because of the paparazzi? Was his fear she'd become unable to cope with all the nonsense coming true already? When he'd seen how well she managed? How dignified she was? Or had he got to her by turning down the opportunity to talk over a meal?

His gut instinct was to follow her back to her apartment and have it out with her. To get it across to that stubborn mind that he knew what he was doing by staying away, that nothing would ever change, and that eventually she'd get fed up and leave him.

He would not be telling her he'd barely slept all week for thinking about her, and missing her in his arms. There'd be no mention of wanting to propose to her and have a real family life with the woman he adored so much. No, he'd stay away. Today he'd struggled with maintaining his aloof façade. Hell, it had been impossible not to smile at her a couple of times. But that was where it had to end.

He pulled his car key from his pocket. Then shoved it back. He wanted to follow Bella home so badly he knew if he got behind the wheel that was exactly what would happen. Which in turn would fuel Fergusson's inquisitiveness. Even Gino might have trouble getting rid of the reporter then. Though Aaron couldn't help the smile that lifted his mouth. Probably not. Gino was a force to be reckoned with and when it came to looking out for his sister there'd be no holding him back.

He needed to be like that himself when it came to Bella and look out for her, stop worrying about his heart so much. He'd been protecting her by keeping his distance, but maybe he'd only made it worse because now Fergusson wanted to unravel the puzzle that to him was Aaron Marshall and Bella Rosso. Aaron stared at his feet. Had he blown the one real chance of happiness he'd had in years? He should fight for Bella, not against her. He needed to fight for both of them, for their future. Damn it.

First he had a phone call to make.

When that was done he got into his car and headed to the Rosso apartments. It was time to sort this out, to lay everything out so Bella totally understood why they couldn't be together.

Or he could go home and sit on the deck and watch the sun go down on another grotty day.

Or he could lay his heart on the line, show Bella how much he loved her, and ask for her forgiveness and another chance to make her happy. To make *them* happy.

There really wasn't an option.

Bella sat at the family table alongside her *mamma* and stirred her spaghetti round and round with a fork. Her appetite had vanished along with Aaron. Even Sophia was quieter than usual.

Mamma nudged her with an elbow. 'You've got a visitor. We'd better make a space for him.'

'Come in, Aaron.' Gino was already bringing a chair over. 'You sit with Bella.'

Gino hadn't asked her much about what was going on, but that didn't mean he wasn't aware they were having problems. He was setting Aaron up so he couldn't walk away. Gino liked Aaron a lot. That didn't mean he'd let him away with anything though. 'It's seafood spaghetti tonight.'

'Is this all right with you, Bella?' Aaron asked.

'Didn't I invite you to dinner?' Her heart was hammering. The fork slipped out of her fingers with a clatter. He'd come. What had changed his mind? Swallowing a big mouthful of sparkling water, she held onto all the questions buzzing in her head. No point in scaring him off before he'd sat down.

He sank onto the chair and looked directly at her. 'I'm sorry.'

For what? 'We'll talk later. Enjoy dinner first, and relax amongst the family. They've missed you.' It had only been two weeks, but they were the longest weeks she'd known in a while.

Aaron blinked and looked around. 'Hello, everyone.'

And just like that all the chatter started up again with everyone talking over each other. Aaron slowly relaxed and joined in the noise as though there'd never been a glitch in their relationship.

Gino placed a large bowl in front of him

with a clap on his back. 'Get that into you,' he ordered.

Bella forked up a mouthful from the mess she'd made in her bowl and munched away happily. Whatever Aaron had come to talk about didn't matter right now. He was here, and that was what was important. It was a start.

Later, when they sat on her deck with coffee at hand, she wondered if she'd expected too much. Aaron had gone quiet on her again. 'Don't do this,' she said.

'I don't know where to start,' he admitted. 'I don't want to make a bigger mess than I already have.'

'Try the beginning. It usually works.'

'When I was qualifying in emergency medicine I did a term in New Zealand where I met Amy. We fell in love and got engaged. It was wonderful. Then we went to London and the fun began. Mum was getting continuous attention from the media over a movie that hit the screen big time, and Dad was hitting the headlines daily about a murder case he'd ruled on. In other words, it was the usual world for my family. At first Amy coped, but slowly she began withdrawing. The worst was her pulling back from our relationship. Then one day she upped and left, went home to Auckland. I flew down to see her and tried to rectify our engagement but she shunned me, said she never wanted a part in my family again. Within six months Amy was married to her childhood sweetheart and having a baby.'

Bella reached for his hand, and held tight. She couldn't imagine how that had felt. No doubt beyond painful. 'No wonder you're afraid to love again.'

'You always read me too easily.'

'The thing is, Aaron, it's not hard to know where you're coming from. I loved Jason so much I've always believed I'd never be that lucky again. Some people don't know the kind of love I've had, and to think I'd find it again was beyond comprehension. That's why I was reticent.'

'Your honesty doesn't leave room for manoeuvre.'

'You want me to sugar coat it?'

He shook his head and smiled. 'Not likely. I haven't finished what I want to tell you.' He sipped his coffee. 'The way you've handled the media over the last few days makes me hope you wouldn't walk away when the horrendous days occur. But I've seen this before. I know how Amy was ground down so quickly. I am afraid of that happening again.'

'Are you saying you'd like a relationship with me?' Her hands were shaking and she pulled away from his grip.

'What I'm getting around to telling you, Bella Rosso, is that I am so in love with you it hurts not to be with you all the time. I want to risk everything for you. I can't not take the chance because to walk away from you would undermine everything I believe in.'

'Which is?' she whispered.

'Love.'

Love. There it was. One word said it all. 'I love you so much, Aaron. I want to share my life with you. To share my daughter and my family. Everything I have.'

'Love, Bella.' He was standing, reaching down for her, lifting her up into his arms, holding her fiercely as well as gently, and then he was kissing her as though he'd never stop.

Sinking into him, she let go the last worries that they might be making a big mistake and took a chance on for ever. Love for ever. Aaron in her life for ever.

Then he was pulling back, but she trusted him. He wasn't about to say he'd made a mistake.

'Bella, I'll also be there for Sophia all the way, will try to be the best dad I can.'

'I never had any doubts.' He was kind and caring, and what more could she ask for when it came to her daughter? 'You'll make a great *papà*. The best.'

'Will you marry me?'

'Yes. Try and stop me.' She stretched up to kiss him some more. No such thing as too much of those lips.

Loud clapping interrupted them from down on the restaurant veranda, followed by shouts and laughter.

'Get down here so we can celebrate with a bottle of the best champagne in the house.' Gino of course.

Bella grinned. She hadn't felt this good in such a long time. 'Welcome to the family.'

'Guess your father isn't so good at keeping promises.' Aaron laughed as he took her hand.

'What do you mean?'

'I went and saw your father before I came into the restaurant. Asked him if he minded if I proposed to his daughter. Looks like he's told everybody.'

Papà would be stoked. 'You're more Italian than many men I know.' Then she couldn't resist asking, 'What would you have done if he'd said no?'

Aaron laughed. 'Talked him into saying yes.'

'Come on, you two. The champagne's getting warm.' Gino again.

As if. 'I'm going to have a very small glass of that. I am not going to miss celebrating my engagement to the sexiest, loving man in my life.'

Kick, kick.

Bella drew a breath, and took Aaron's hand to hold it over her belly. 'Sophia approves. That's the hardest kick in a week.'

'Hi, Sophia. Looks like we're going to be a family. What do you think?'

Kick.

'No more questions, please. That was too hard.' Bella grinned.

'One more thing,' Aaron said.

'What?'

'I'm taking over Giuseppe's role in the ED three days a week. I'm going to find a part-time job in Milano as well to keep up to date with any changes that happen in emergency medicine.'

'This couldn't get any better.' Bella laughed as she dragged her fiancé out of the apartment and downstairs to join the family.

EPILOGUE

Restaurant Closed for Family Celebration

'DON'T KEEP QUIET about the wedding, will you, Gino?' Bella muttered happily as she looked at the large sign her brothers had hung on the gate that morning.

So much for keeping her wedding a small affair that only family and friends knew about. But then again, with the Marshall clan involved it was never going to be a secret. The media were already hanging around outside the property, kept there by manners, and when those were ignored by the pushier reporters the security company Aaron had hired quietly dealt with them.

Despite all that she couldn't be happier. She'd found love for a second time, and Aaron had settled into life in Stresa as if he was always meant to be here. His nightmares had all but vanished, and he'd obtained the perfect two-day-a-week job in Milano's largest hospital. Now they were getting married and soon Sophia would arrive.

'You ready, Bella?' Her father stood in the apartment's doorway, dressed to the nines in a three-piece suit, and looking so proud.

'Yes, Papà, I'm ready.' She'd been ready since the moment Aaron proposed. Slipping her arm through Papà's, she looked over her shoulder to her sisters-in-law. 'Come on, let's get me married.'

A gentle kick reminded her there was more excitement to come in a couple of weeks. She'd wanted to wait until Sophia was born before having the wedding, but Maggie was on a short break from LA at the moment and so they'd brought the date forward so she'd be able to attend. Rubbing her tummy, Bella whispered, 'You're still coming to the wedding, darling. Just not quite how we'd planned it.'

'You look beautiful,' Aaron said, his eyes full of love, as she walked up the makeshift aisle between endless vases of roses.

He still stole her breath away. Just like that

very first time she'd laid eyes on him. When she reached him, she stretched up and kissed him.

'Hold on,' Papà growled. 'I haven't given you away yet.'

Everyone laughed, and she told the marriage celebrant good-naturedly to get on with the job.

He obliged, and within minutes Bella's *papà* was sitting down beside Mamma and wiping his eyes as his daughter became Aaron's wife.

'I love you,' Bella whispered to her new husband.

'Same back at you.' Aaron swung her up into his arms and kissed her hard.

'That's enough, you two. Let's go celebrate.' Gino had all his chefs working in the kitchen and they came out to toast the couple before heading back to finish preparing the four-course meal.

Three hours later, Bella leaned back in her chair, holding her breath as a sharp pain shot through her abdomen. 'No way. You can't turn up today, Sophia.'

'You all right?' Aaron asked.

'I think so.' Was this the beginning of her

labour or just a harder than usual nudge from her daughter to let her know she wasn't going to be forgotten during the celebrations?

Ten minutes later Bella had her answer. 'We're not going on our honeymoon,' she gasped.

'What?' Aaron's eyes widened when he noticed her clutching her stomach. 'You're kidding, right?'

'You think so?'

'No, I don't.' He stood up, sat down, looking confused. 'What now?'

She laughed. 'Carry on as we were, at least until the contractions are closer.'

Twelve hours later, Bella gave a final push and Sophia arrived in the world.

The midwife wrapped her daughter in a small blanket and placed her on Bella's breast. 'There you go. She's lovely.'

Bella swallowed the tears clogging her throat and kissed Sophia's brow. 'Hello, sweetheart. You are gorgeous.'

Her husband sat on the edge of the bed beside her, his eyes full of tears and love. 'She certainly is.'

'Sophia, meet Papà.' Bella placed their daughter in Aaron's arms, her heart expanding with every breath she took. She had got lucky again. 'I love you both,' she whispered.

* * * * *

LET'S TALK

Romance

For exclusive extracts, competitions and special offers, find us online:

MillsandBoon

@MillsandBoon

@MillsandBoonUK

@MillsandBoonUK

Get in touch on 01413 063 232

For all the latest titles coming soon, visit
millsandboon.co.uk/nextmonth